COVID ONE NINE

Stories and Poems

Edited by Ibiso Graham-Douglas

Copyright 2024

Covik One Nine © Ibiso Graham-Douglas
ISBN 9798875575372

Smoke and Ashes © Dolapo Marinho; The Good Doctor © Olukorede S. Yishau; God Abeg © Ibiso Graham-Douglas; Aproko © Michael Afenfia; © Shehu Zock-Sock;
Original of the Species © Chimeka Garricks; Captured Moments © Michael W. Ndiomu;
Wuhan Is Next Door, Oxford Fellowship in Limbo, and We Shall Rise © Obari Gomba.

The authors have been identified as the owners of the works contained in this book as asserted to them by the copyright laws.

Published by
Paperworth Books Limited
Nigeria
+2348023130116
www.paperworthbooks.com
info@paperworthbooks.com

A catalogue record of this book is available from the National Library of Nigeria. All rights reserved. No part of this publication may be reproduced, transmitted, or saved in a retrieval system, in any form or by any means, without written permission from the authors.

*For my mother,
Her Excellency Hon Dr Bolere Elizabeth Ketebu
who is deeply missed every day.*

For John, Diweni, and the thousands of lives lost to COVID-19 in Nigeria, both recorded and unrecorded.

Edited by Ibiso Graham-Douglas

Contents

Wuhan is Next Door *Obari Gomba*	7
Smoke and Ashes *Dolapo Marinho*	9
The Good Doctor *Olukorede S. Yishau*	29
God Abeg *Ibiso Graham-Douglas*	46
Aproko *Michael Afenfia*	65
Oxford Fellowship in Limbo *Obari Gomba*	85
Heavy *Shehu Zock-Sock*	87
Original of the Species *Chimeka Garricks*	109
Captured Moments *Michael W. Ndiomu*	132
We Shall Rise *Obari Gomba*	159
Editor's Note	161
Acknowledgements	162

COVIK ONE NINE

Edited by Ibiso Graham-Douglas

Wuhan is Next Door

Obari Gomba

(*For Li Wenliang*)

THE STORY WAS A SNAKE THAT SLITHERED
out of a WeChat group.

You cannot keep a viral snake
in a bag that has a hole.
You cannot keep a problem
in a room that has many exits.

The chat room had open ears, some in sync
with the ears of the state.
The story was a snake that coiled
around a city; a city ignored the truth
because its head was in a gutter.

In the days that followed,
time sat between the thighs
of zoonosis, the secrecy of science,
a market, and a leaky lab.

But no one knew what everyone
ought to know, and the whistleblower
died. Lights were off for five minutes.

Whistles were blown for the ordinary hero.
Then the snake sped around the world
because Wuhan was just next door
to all of us.

Wuhan is still next door.

Obari Gomba (PhD), *winner of both the Nigeria Prize for Literature and the PAWA Prize for African Poetry, is an Honorary Fellow in Writing of the University of Iowa (USA) and the Associate Dean of Humanities at the University of Port Harcourt (Nigeria). He has been the TORCH Global South Visiting Professor and Visiting Fellow at All Souls College, University of Oxford (UK). He is a two-time winner of the Best Literary Artiste Award and the First Prize for Drama of the English Association of the University of Nigeria, Nsukka. His works include* Guerrilla Post *(Winner of ANA Drama Prize),* For Every Homeland *(Winner of ANA Poetry Prize),* Thunder Protocol *(Winner of ANA Poetry Prize), among others.*

Edited by Ibiso Graham-Douglas

Smoke and Ashes

Dolapo Marinho

Something about the way she sits crumpled in the last pew makes me pay attention—the downward slope of her shoulders, the quiet sobbing, the dark glasses. I stand watching her from the entrance of the church. She is conspicuous by her neutrality, no *aso-ebi*, no *gele*, no family. I watch as she holds her children tight, one boy fidgeting with the knee rest, a girl asleep on her lap. The boy's ears are unusual, low set, pinned back.
Gboye.
"Mum, let's go to the front."
Priscilla's voice cuts into my thoughts. I allow her to clasp her hand in mine, pull me across the threshold and into the church. The contrast of our skin is striking. Hers is supple, youthful, hopeful.

My arrival causes a stir, as some of the people Gboye and I shared our lives with stand up to greet me. We could not invite all our loved ones, the government directive stated no more than fifty per cent capacity. Had we been able to, the church would have overflowed. My husband was so indiscriminating and generous with his friendship. It drove me mad sometimes.

The banner at the church entrance has Gboye's face beaming out to the world. My heart constricts because I know he would hate it.

"No fanfare when I die. Just burn me and sprinkle my ashes in the Lagoon." He had said many a time. A doctor so used to death becomes unsentimental about its significance, unmoved by the symbology that keeps those left behind tethered to sanity. I could not obey his wishes. I needed a place to go, a visual reminder that he had spent time on this Earth.

As I look up towards the altar, I see them all spaced out along the pews, our nearest and dearest, social but distant. Unable to hug nor comfort one another. Their faces are hidden behind a myriad surgical masks. Some of them go as far back as our university days, when Gboye and I caused quite a stir when we announced we would be making our lives in Lagos. They thought we would have no future here, that few would accept us. And yet, they, too, trickled home in the end.

It's a bittersweet feeling that Gboye's parents are not here. The taboo against knowing the final resting place of one's child makes a sad day even sadder. Even if tradition had granted them permission to come, the virus that claimed their only son's life would have made it too risky. As I look up at the chandeliers hanging down from the vaulted ceiling, I struggle with the thought that part of the reason I have decided on a church funeral is to show his parents that his choice of wife has not been a complete disaster.

The woman's head shoots up at the stirring among the crowd. In a panic, she clumsily raises the sleeping child onto her shoulder, grips the boy's hand tight and quickly makes her way out of the church.

She is slight of frame, dark-skinned, average height. Not even her eyes are visible above the black surgical mask that shrouds her face in mystery. A dove-grey chiffon boubou slinks over her slim body. She is graceful, broken.

I let go of Priscilla's hand, give her my purse and whisper for her to take her seat. I feel my breath constrict in my lungs as I run after the woman. I do not know why, but I feel an urgent need to meet this stranger, to engage.

"Stop."

She freezes at the sound of my voice. The little boy gazes back at me. His eyes are wide-set, piercing. Familiar.

"I don't want any trouble." Her voice is low, rigid back facing me.

"Then why have you come?"

She hesitates but then begins to turn around. She has taken her glasses off and her mask now sits on her chin. I see her face is a crisscross of tear tracks.

"Because I loved him, and he loved us."

It feels like a cat is clawing at the back of my neck. The confidence in her voice leaves me cold. But then just a half hour ago, I would have said the same. I would have screamed to the universe that Gboye loved me beyond life itself. That against all the odds, I was his and he was mine, in totality.

She moves her arm to adjust the child's position on her shoulder and I smell the unmistakable, *Cool Water* muskiness that has been the indelible scent of my pillows, for the past quarter of a century. Gboye.

We stand in silence outside the back entrance of the church, hidden from view. Only the cleaners, ushers, drivers and late-comers use this side. A young man walks by with his mop and bucket, his eyes linger on me as he offers up a low greeting. Neither of us respond. Our energy is being used to shoulder the weight of what must come next.

"Mummy, I want to wee-wee." The boy. A superhero child mask muffles his voice. He has almond eyes and dense lashes. I adjust my gaze to take him in. He is well put together, loved. Eight, maybe nine years old, I reckon.

"GB, not now, please." His mother admonishes him, but she pulls him closer to her. I blink.

"GB?" She knows what I am asking and bites her lip before answering.

"Gboyega." Her eyes lower, "Junior."

I nod. Saliva floods my mouth. Gboyega Junior. I am swimming in a wave of nausea and have to clench my butt cheeks to keep steady on my feet. It seems implausible but I understand what has happened. Gboye went in search of the one thing I could not give him—children of his own. Priscilla was not enough, not his progeny. Adoption is not reproduction. I look intently at the three people before me and rage begins to bubble beneath my skin. I should have let her walk away.

A driver blares his horn at a pure water seller that has jumped into the road in front of him. The brutal, jarring noise brings relief from the knives slashing every nerve in my body. I see a woman wandering from car window to car window, fingers bunched against a filthy, light blue surgical mask. A baby wearing a woollen bonnet is strapped into the small of her back. The child's head lolls disconcertingly every time she moves towards a new car. Heat rises up my legs, sweat trickles down the inside of my thighs.

An old, unwelcome sensation spreads in the pit of my stomach. One I have worked obscenely hard to control. A lowering into the dark corridors that form labyrinths inside my head. A vice grip of despair tightens around my chest. If left unchecked, it will cause me to howl. I am so afraid of returning to that place, my teeth begin to chatter.

"Like I said, Belinda, I didn't come here to make trouble. I don't want anything from you or..."

"Shut your mouth."

She stiffens. My words are like a slap to her face. Who does this woman think she is, using my name like we are acquainted? My head is engorged with hatred. I want to grab her by the neck and squeeze. Push her into the road and watch as she is flung in the air and crushed under the weight of my fury. More words tumble from my mouth.

"Whore! You don't want anything from me?"

Tremors take possession of my limbs, "But you already took all that was mine, everything I cared for and thought was real." I am thunderous with bitterness. "You and your bastard children came here to destroy me."

I wipe away the rash of perspiration that has formed across my upper lip and glare at her. The mask I have been holding now crushed inside my fist. I unfurl it, my vision a blurry haze. I stare at the crescent-shaped string, the pleated, rectangular cloth that was supposed to save us from the greedy, airborne disease that has forced the entire world onto its knees.

I suddenly feel naked. Bereft and violated by my own husband. The man I loved with every fibre of my being. And yet he is the perpetrator of a betrayal so enormous I am a single step from walking into the road. Away from his funeral and the vulgar violence of being confronted by his mistress.

What a laughingstock you must be, Belinda. Bi-widowed by COVID-19 and this evil wench of a woman with her children fathered by deception. I cast my mind back inside the church. All the faces that rose to greet me. My support system, my tribe, our dear friends of uncountable years. How many of them knew? What number harboured the lie with Gboye? Which of them sat at my table, drank my wine, yet knew the truth as we dined? Had they ever truly accepted me? The distress is unbearable.

I spit forcefully onto the ground, inches from her feet. She does not flinch. I sway, disjointed and adrift. I no longer recognise myself, cannot regulate my thoughts or grasp the previous narrative of my life. Everything is slipping through my fingers. I look up when I realise the pain in my hand is from my fingernails digging into my palm. A steeliness crosses the woman's face. She smiles and inhales deeply. I notice it is not a mocking smile. The child at her shoulder stirs.

"Gboyega always said we were similar."

He talked to her about me? I am blindsided by this piece of information, blistered by the ferocity of its implication. The sun sits directly above our heads, air thick with moisture. I exhale. I have never gotten used to this tropical heat.

Satisfied at having landed her blow and before I can restore my composure, she continues, "He said you were as tough as they come. That your mind was the most amazing he had ever encountered." A dry chuckle. "I always envied his admiration of you."

My breathing has become constricted again. My inhaler is in the bag that I handed to Priscilla. I suck air into my nostrils. I was a topic of conversation in their sordid love nest. Gboye, I did not see this coming. After everything we went through. I feel almost grateful that this ended you. For this crime, I would have covered your head with a pillow and smothered the life out of you.

We lock eyes and stay rigid for what feels like an age. The wind picks up and her boubou flaps, lending her the air of a bird. I notice a vein snaking down the middle of her forehead, crow's feet concertina the side of each eye. She wears no make-up or earrings, yet her beauty is difficult to deny. I do not even know her name. She stands immobile, a hurricane sucking up my air.

"Mummy..." GB is moving from one leg to the other.

He breaks the spell. His mother strokes his arm in assurance. I had forgotten the boy's presence and immediately feel flushed with shame. The child with Gboye's eyes seems distressed. A flutter ripples across my chest.

"The toilet block is just behind you." I point to the low building to her right. The woman's face softens. She adjusts her sleeping child again.

"Thank you. GB, go to the toilet. Remember, don't sit. Wash your hands very well."

He nods and skips away. We both follow him with our eyes until the door closes behind him.

"Trying to teach him independence." She offers the reason for not going in with him.

I do not respond.

"It's not easy being a mother. You're scared all the time..." She catches herself. "I'm sorry, Belinda... I didn't mean..."

I turn away from her judging eyes.

The church bells begin to chime, announcing the arrival of the Clergy. We stand in the burning sun, the silence screaming a million words. My skin singes, Lagos whirs around us but we are separated from the madness. Cocooned inside a chrysalis from a parallel reality. It is strange to think that just a few moments ago I had a completely different life. The way the universe toys with its inhabitants, one second all is well, the next you have fallen off track and are hurtling at speed along an unanticipated trajectory, broken within and without.

The wind picks up again. I brush hair away from my face, tuck it behind my ears. It has thinned out over the years. I wonder what will become of this woman now that Gboye is gone. What security he left her, any plans he made. All this time I thought I was his entire world. The guilt I carried for so long at not being able to give him a child. But Gboye was already basking in fatherhood. Had been for years. It all makes sense now. The change in him that I thought was due to Priscilla's presence in our lives. The calmness, patience. I believed I had been the problem solver, that my happiness at finally becoming a mother had granted him peace. How wrong I was, how deluded. Priscilla was for me alone. Gboye had created his own solution. One man, two lives.

I peer at the little girl as she squirms. I cannot tell her age. She seems small for a toddler, too large to be a baby. She too, is an innocent enmeshed in this madness. I feel my rage beginning to subside.

"There's a bench under the carport. You should get her out of the sun."

The woman turns her head in the direction of my pointed finger. A finger covered in freckles, brown spots. I notice her button nose, elegant profile and see what Gboye must have found attractive. Her carriage is graceful, movement confident. Her skin is blemish free, aglow with perspiration. I feel old beside her.

I do not know why, but I explain as we walk that the drivers usually use the carport on Sundays, but since the pandemic began, few people have been coming to church. Gboye and I had also shied away from attending service, preferring to sing our hearts out on the sofa as online church streamed into our home.

The woman searches my face as she says, "Thank you."

Indignation sets my face in stone. I have questions.

She settles onto the bench.

"What's her name?"

"Josephine. Gboyega wanted to name her after you but that was too strange for me. So, I agreed to your middle name."

My thighs begin to tremble again and more out of necessity than desire, I lower myself onto the bench next to her. I struggle to comprehend what is happening or if any of this is even real. Could my grief at Gboye's death have finally fractured my mind? Have I actually been sectioned again and am simply wallowing in some drug-induced hallucination? My life seems fastened to skates, hurtling down the side of a mountain to a destination unknown. I need to steady myself, have to make it all make sense.

I adjust my body and turn slightly towards her. My expression a smorgasbord of conflicting emotions. Questions in my mind read like screen credits. But I suddenly find myself unable to speak. I am navigating a nightmare of such proportions my brain cannot compute.

She seems to sense the hopelessness that submerges me.

"My name is Olamide." She pauses to see if I want her to continue. I say nothing, press my lips together and fix my eyes on the horizon. I can see the security staff ushering guests towards parking spaces. The church must be filling up. They must all be wondering where I am.

"This is not the way I wanted you to find out. Gboyega wanted to tell you but..."

"How long?" I only want facts, no insights, no sentiment. She doesn't hesitate.

"Nine years."

We stew in the loudness of the number. She wasn't a fling.

"Honestly, it began as a regrettable mistake. I was a trainee nurse at the hospital, and we sometimes worked nights..."

She keeps talking but my mind is deep in the past. Nine years ago. When I had the miscarriage. By then we had been trying for a baby for years.

"...he was so afraid you wouldn't come out of the depression..."

At the lowest point in my life, the great Dr Gboyega Adeyoye was sleeping with his nurse. O Lord, so cliché, so cheap. Vomit scorches the back of my throat.

"It was nothing, meant nothing... at first."

I'm right back in that hospital room. I can still see the doctor's mouth moving even though I have stopped hearing his words. I remember him telling us we would probably never have children. The best thing for me was a full hysterectomy. The BEST thing... a hysterectomy. Surely that was the worst. His words were devastating in their efficiency, a samurai sword precisely wielded to sever all links with hope.

Gboye asked questions, medical ones, practical ones. Could the eggs be harvested? Frozen? How long for recovery? All I could wonder was the number of women who had already sat in my seat that day. Staring up with optimism only to have to digest the doctor's stone-faced "best" option. Countless women told their body was unfit for purpose. "Best" to remove the delusion entirely. I remember the painful comfort of my nails scratching deep into the skin of my arm—the redness against the pallor. Blood drained from it in horror. I feel Gboye's arm around my shoulder, his muskiness saturating my nostrils as I cry into his chest.

"...but then I fell pregnant."

I snap back to the present. On the wind sits the smell of smoke burning in the distance. It is acrid and makes me cough.

"Are you okay?" Olamide asks. At least I now know her name.

"Fine." I look at her. Her eyes are concerned, so I add, "Thank you."

Gboyega Junior comes bounding out of the toilet. He jumps up and sits in the space between us. He turns to look at me. From the way his eyes reduce to slits, I can tell he's smiling.

"Did you wash your hands?"

"Yes, Mummy. Can I have Ribena?"

Olamide glances up at me.

"Gboyega was always anti-sweet things. Thought it would damage his teeth. I'm more about moderation."

Yes, that sounds like the Gboye I know. Knew. A stickler in all things. Serious and principled. Inexplicably, I chuckle.

"He was certainly passionate about his principles," I say.

Olamide bears her teeth in a wide smile. She has a gold cap on one of her incisors.

"There was one time a patient wanted to discharge himself against the doctor's advice. I was pleading with the man not to go. Gboyega walked past on his rounds and simply asked the man if he knew what he was doing..."

As Olamide speaks, she deftly uses one hand to open the shoulder bag she has lifted to her knees and takes out a triangular-shaped pack of Ribena.

"...the man insisted on leaving, so Gboyega printed off the consent forms, got the man to sign and wished him luck."

GB takes the Ribena from his mum and thanks her. He plunges the straw into the silver hole, pulls down his Spider-Man mask and begins to suck up the purple liquid.

With his face now fully exposed, his likeness to his father is uncomfortable.

"When I asked why he hadn't tried to make the sick man stay. He just said the greatest dignity a man has is his ability to make his own choices."

Olamide has a faraway look on her face as though she is remembering something painful. She too, must be in agony. The child on her shoulder shrieks. I watch as she lowers her, Josephine, into the crook of her arm. Something is not quite right. She seems too sleepy. As I peer closer at the baby, I hear Priscilla's voice over my shoulder.

"I've been looking everywhere for you, Mummy. The priest wants to see you."

Priscilla is breathless. She assesses the scene and does a shallow curtsey in Olamide's direction.

"Good morning, ma."

"Good morning, my dear." Olamide beams up at Priscilla.

Priscilla returns the smile and glances down at the little boy sandwiched between us. Soon enough, seeds of confusion begin to germinate on her face. At the same time, there is only recognition on Olamide's own. Of course, Gboye has told her about the child we adopted seven years ago.

The memory smokes into my mind. We had gone to the orphanage to adopt a newborn foundling. As usual, our presence had caused a stir. The children had surrounded us, they were trying to stroke my hair. It was down to my back in those days and dyed bright red. I'd promised myself not to cut it until I fell pregnant.

Priscilla had welcomed us while deftly ushering the curious children away. She was already twelve, with little prospect of ever being chosen by a family. One of the carers saw me watching Priscilla and explained that the older ones usually ended up institutionalised. Often becoming staff members themselves, looking after the new intakes. I could see that she was warm and smart, with an electric smile that sadness had turned down at the edges. I felt an energy emanating from Priscilla that I wanted to be close to. A recognition of suffering, and yet, resilience. I followed her with my eyes as she played with the smaller children, enquired about our comfort and assisted the older carers. I remember squeezing Gboye's arm and the quizzical look he gave me when I suggested an older child. This older child, Priscilla. He wasn't convinced, and we quarrelled on the car journey home.

"We agreed on a baby, Bee." The crease between his eyebrows deepening.

"I know, but she just feels right for our family."

"How? She's old. Already living with traumas we might not be able to cope with."

"And who isn't?"

"My point exactly."

We fall into silence. The kind that has begun to plague us since the hysterectomy, noiseless minutes searching for words that never come. The hum of the car engine amplifies the void.

"Did you see how good she was with the other children? How kind her spirit is?"

Gboye says nothing. I sigh.

"I... I just feel like an actual baby will be too much of a reminder that we can never have our own."

I glance quickly at him. His knuckles pop as he grips the steering wheel. A visible pulse in his cheek as he clenches and unclenches his jaw. I persevere.

"Priscilla will be a companion for us, without the heartache... and stinky nappies."

He gives me a half smile and side eye that melts my heart. Thick lashes, dark lips. I want to squash him into my chest, breathe him deep inside my lungs.

"Mummy, are you okay?"

My mind clears. Priscilla is squatting in front of me, holding my hand. She carries a worried, intense look the same way she did when we found out Gboye had died from COVID. Hard to imagine that was just ten days ago when both our worlds came crashing down. I still don't know what I would have done without her. She is the blessing I knew she would be. It isn't until Priscilla wipes them away that I feel the tears streaming down my face.

GB, his mother and Priscilla are all staring at me. I feel the flush in my face, sniff up the mucus streaming out of my nose.

Suddenly, Olamide begins to gather her things.

"I should go." She says, adjusting the bag strap onto one shoulder and returning the baby to the other. "Coming here was a mistake..."

"No." It's a whisper but audible enough to make her stop what she is doing.

I squeeze Priscilla's hand, give her a reassuring smile and say, "I'll come and see the priest soon. Tell him I'm attending to something."

Priscilla hesitates. She wants to protect me from this stranger who has clearly punched perforations in my life story. She's old enough to know what has happened and I feel the force field of love radiating from her in my direction.

I look her straight in the eye and nod. She leaves after a final glance at GB. The church bells rings again. This time the chime is continuous. Gboye's hearse has arrived.

"Stay, please." My voice is weak, drained of all emotion. I have lost the energy to fight. Even though she knew about me, Gboye made victims of us both with his selfishness. It would be wrong to take out my wrath on this woman and her children when the person who has caused this pain is already dead. I ask her not to go. Instead, we should walk to the church together. Sit at the front and pay our final respects to Gboye.

Olamide falters. She tells GB to go and play, once again our eyes follow the little boy. His relief at being released is palpable. For the first time she looks beaten, defeated. Her earlier defiance has given way to tiredness. I realise she now has a lot on her hands, two small children, the man she loved, dead. My own twenty-five-year marriage is already erasing itself from my head. I find it difficult to recall Gboye's face, his voice, his smile. How is it possible to live with another for so long and have no inkling of what they are capable of?

"I'm pregnant again."

This time her words do not sting. I recognised the waddle as we walked to the bench earlier. The pendulous sway of a woman with child. I do not think there is anything she can reveal to me now that would cause me greater hurt. My heart has already popped.

Olamide becomes intense. Her furtive eyes try to settle on something but can't. She avoids looking at me and her leg bobs up and down like a piston. The baby in her arm remains asleep, lulled by the rocking. She has a cleft palate. That is what makes her face striking. There is a gap in her upper lip where the two sides do not meet.

Olamide follows my gaze to her baby's face.

"She has cerebral palsy." She smiles weakly, "Sometimes, I wonder if she is punishment for what Gboye and I have done."

She suddenly turns to face me, her words come like a storm.

"Belinda... I have to tell you something. Gboye was devastated every day by what he did to you."

I smirk.

"He would cry at the thought of you finding out... he just didn't know how to make it right."

She stares intently at me. "This baby is yours."

I look at the child in her arms.

"No, the one in here." She reaches for my hand and lays it on her abdomen. It is fuller than I realised, warm. What is this woman talking about?

"It was supposed to be a gift."

Confusion is etched upon my face.

"He asked me to be a surrogate. To give you what you always wanted. A child of your own. So we used one of your fertilised embryos, and I took in."

I begin to shake my head. Slowly at first and then more frenzied. The more I shake my head the more blurred the world becomes. I feel a torrent of noise rise from my gut up my throat and out my mouth. I scream at the injustice, the total disrespect. I howl to the heavens at how much of a lie my life with Gboye had been. I begin to run.

"BELINDA!"

I hear Olamide scream my name, but it is too late. I am already in the road. I see the horror on the bus driver's face. The slow, devastating realisation that he will be unable to stop in time, that my body will be crushed. I spread out my arms and welcome the impact. It is a worthless body anyway.

****

"Welcome back. We thought we lost you." The man's voice is familiar. Deep.

I try to prise my eyes open. They are sticky and sore, like Velcro. I struggle to regain my focus. I hear beeping noises and feel a tight strap around my face. The fluorescent lighting makes my eyes water. My throat feels raw. A shadow comes into view. Blurred face, smiling. A man. I try to speak, but a thousand nails pinprick my throat. I feel as though I am underwater. I cannot keep my eyes open.

When I try to open my eyes again, they are less sore. My chest feels like an elephant has trampled all over it. My breathing is laboured but my throat feels less gravelly. I try to move my hand but it is leaden. Try to clench my fist but it is such an effort I become winded. I concentrate on regaining my breath and stare up at the ceiling. Brown islands of water stains float above me from leaks in the roof.

Cobwebs hang low from the cornices, dense with dust. The smell of bleach is cloying.

Where is Priscilla? What happened?

I move my eyes to the right. They hurt so much I see starbursts but I can see enough to know that I am not alone. There are others around me, also lying supine.

"You are awake, ma." Her face eclipses the light. She is wearing a hospital-grade mask, face shield and gloves. She has a plastic apron on over her nurse's uniform. "You really fought."

I take three deep breaths. The air that fills my lungs is pure and sweet. A lifetime of asthma has taught me to recognise oxygen from a tank. With all the energy I can muster, I ask, "The funeral?" It is a hoarse whisper and she leans in to hear better.

"Funeral..." I say again.

She does not understand me because all she says is, "The doctor will do his rounds soon. He will be very happy to see you awake." She checks the fluid bag attached to my drip, writes something down on her clipboard and moves on to the next bed.

My head is sore. Flashes of memories come back. The funeral. A woman, young boy. I try to form images around them, but they slip away as quickly as they appear. My eyes close again.

When I come to, I hear two people talking at the foot of my bed. I keep my eyes closed and concentrate. Despite the oxygen, I still find it hard to breathe.

"Mrs Belinda Adeyoye. There's still fluid in her lungs but she's responding well."

"Vitals?"

"Close to normal... still weak."

The doctor flicks the pages on the clipboard up before continuing.

"Lucky woman."

"Continue with IV?" The nurse asks.

"Yes. Also, keep on oxygen for the next few hours. She's BUPA, right?"

"Yes, sir."

"Have you notified the British High Commission she has regained consciousness?"

"I have, Sir."

"Thank God. It will be bad for a foreigner to die at our hospital."

They continue to talk as they move away from my bed.

"What of the other lady they brought in with her?" The doctor flips his sheets again. "The one that pushed her out of the way and got hit by the bus."

"They rejected her at reception for lack of funds. But one lady paid for the operation."

"Who did the surgery?"

"It was supposed to be Dr Fola, but the woman died in prep. Her children are sitting with the young lady, I think they called her Priscilla, in reception."

"Next of kin?"

"We're still trying to locate them."

Tears pool inside the crevices of my ears.

The End.

Dolapo Marinho *is a writer and director who has always been fascinated by the power words possess to hurt, heal and haunt. Growing up in a large, dynamic family, she became convinced that blame was the root cause of most relationship crises. By* *dissecting human interactions through this lens, characters emerge in her mind, and her words bring their stories to life. Her debut novel will be released in 2024.*

Edited by Ibiso Graham-Douglas

The Good Doctor

Olukorede S. Yishau

When my father and mother were flogging me out of the magnificent palace, Nadia was with them, smiling as though she was deriving joy from my ordeal. They were meticulous in their act of wickedness. At some point, I saw sadness when she noticed the beating wasn't changing my mind. The pankere canes produced a rhythm similar to the agidigbo drum on my delicate skin.

"Go back! Go back!" They screamed as their pankeres were hitting my body. Their voices were heavy and sounded distinct from what I knew.

"This is not your place," my mother said, striking me on the head with the cane popular among Yoruba parents.

"Get out of here this minute," my father added, doubling the pace of the pankere on my body.

I couldn't cry, I couldn't laugh, I was expressionless.

"Please get him to go back," Nadia said, the smiling now gone replaced by concern.

"He has no choice," my mother said.

"Except he is a bastard," my father agreed with her.

"Of course, he isn't," Mother fought back, becoming more aggressive while applying the pankere on my body.

The more they thrashed me, the more defiant I became. The cane did not affect my body; I had no swelling or blood. It was as though they were caressing and massaging me with the best soothing oil. Suddenly, my father grabbed a hose and began spraying me with the contents, which turned out to be hot water. I screamed and began my journey back.

I woke up and realised it was all a dream, and that was when it made sense to me because my parents could never have subjected me to such punishments, and Nadia would never have derived any shade of joy in my suffering.

Fourteen days had passed before the hot water pulled me out of unconsciousness. Less than an hour later, I went back into a coma and didn't come out of it for another two days when the pungent smell of sanitiser welcomed me. My bones creaked when I tried raising my body, and I couldn't see clearly. As my consciousness improved, I saw at least two machines coaxing me back to the land of the living. I felt something, too, on my arm. An intravenous line was attached to my veins, feeding me with fluids of life. Through my slightly dizzy sight, I saw a nurse dash in and out, only to return with a doctor whose face lit up as soon as he held my gaze.

"Mr Adenola," the doctor's voice carried the distinct melody of a fluent Yoruba speaker.

My mouth felt heavy, so I offered a nod. The doctor checked my vitals and smiled as he recorded his readings in his medical pad. The nurse, who looked Mexican, maintained a vigilant watch over me as though doing otherwise would tilt me back to that halfway place between life and death that I had just returned from.

"What happened?" I finally found my voice.

"You need to rest. All I'll say is that your prognosis is good. We were able to stem the danger right on time. You're a lucky man," the nurse said.

"What danger?"

But neither the doctor nor the nurse answered me. They attached a new IV to my arm, and I soon lost touch with my surroundings again. When I woke up, I tried to remember how I got to the St. Augustus Emergency Hospital from the apartment I shared with my son, Debayo, in Bissonnet. It all seemed like fragments of an elusive dream. But the answer remained on the fringes of memory, like one of those things you had almost remembered but never did.

Debayo helped me connect the dots when Pastor Echeruo was eventually allowed to bring him to see me. His face was covered in a mask, and his feet were encased in non-slip hospital socks to avoid germs that could hurt my weak immune system.

Debayo said he'd found me on the bathroom floor holding my tummy, blood dripping from my mouth. Plenty of blood, he said. The only things that came out of me were weak screams. He said he didn't want to leave me alone but knew he couldn't do much, so he left me and ran to the Leasing Office. He didn't find help there because it was locked. The whole apartment complex was bereft of activities. Everyone was hiding behind the walls, evading the deadly virus.

He said as he cried on his way back, a voice that sounded much like his late mum's told him to go home and dial 911. He ran home and made the call. The dispatcher told him to calm down, asked for our address and assured him help was on its way.

While waiting for the ambulance, he rang our pastor who got to the apartment just as the ambulance took me away.

At this stage, I interrupted him: "I'm really sorry, Debayo. I can imagine what you went through. I couldn't think of another way out. I felt death would save me the shame of failing you."

Debayo just held me, held me really tight and didn't let go until several minutes later after securing an assurance that I would stay with him till God's time.

Pastor Echeruo, who was with us all this time, looked tough and strong, but I saw a hint of wetness somewhere in his eyes. He came close, held my hands with his gloved hands and said silent prayers. He was at it for some minutes. I could hear him speaking in tongues, that part of Christianity I still struggled to understand, a struggle that made me wonder if I wasn't Christian enough because no matter how I tried, I had been unable to speak in tongues, not even when a pastor in Nigeria said he was baptising me with the Holy Spirit. He left me alone after minutes of commanding me to speak, and nothing came out of my mouth.

"It is well, Brother," Pastor Echeruo said. Minutes later, he announced to Debayo that it was time they left. I could sense the fear in my son, the fear of the unknown, the fear of whether or not he would see me again and perhaps the fear of what would follow if I made it out in one piece.

After my son and Pastor Echeruo left, the memory of my life's drama returned in 3D.

****

Until June 2016, I had always believed that Nigeria, Lagos specifically, was the only place for me. London, Singapore, New York and other developed cities held allure as mere travel destinations, and I saw many of them. With a thriving marketing communication firm and two major multibillion naira clients, money was not my problem and spending it was not a challenge.

That June, in my world, cows suddenly no longer mooed, cats stopped meowing, sheep found it hard to bleat, bulls saw bellowing as herculean, ducks quacked no more, donkeys abandoned braying, horses ceased neighing, geese forgot how to cackle, chickens couldn't cluck again, and peacocks no longer fancied screaming when an ownership crises hit my two main clients. I crashed with a loud thud that reverberated all over the industry. My woes were compounded when my third biggest client suddenly cut ties with me.

Amid this, a friend living in the US, my best friend in the university, sold the idea of relocating to America to start all over again. It was a fresh start, he said. I would revamp my business in a country where few cared what I did. Even though people would still ask me for money, they would not likely show up at my door crying, like Nigerians did. He said I could refuse to pick up their calls and blame it on the difference in time zones. Adedeji Lawson piled pressure on me while I was trying to bounce back. The more I tried, the lower I sank into the mud. I started seeing a therapist to help me through the challenging times, and he capitalised on this. He said I would get better therapy in America—especially in Houston.

My Debayo was born in Houston, where we lost his mother, Nadia, from birth complications from our second child. The child, too, did not live.

Raising Debayo, who was a little sickly at birth, was tough. He quickly overcame his recurring health issues and was a precocious child. He met most of his intellectual milestones faster than his peers, even though he was not in the best shape physically. With his mother gone, I became a devoted and patient parent. Nadia had been excellent at raising him. Watching her with him had been reassuring. So, I tried to raise Debayo how I knew Nadia would have wanted. I taught him not to cry when he could say what he wanted; I also told him to always ask questions and never back down until he got an answer he understood. I told him he did not have to agree with the answers he got; he just had to understand what he was told.

After I bowed to the pressure from Adedeji, I sold my remaining two cars and my house in Maryland Estate and told myself not even my bones would return to Nigeria. Adedeji assured me all would be well. He spoke of the elaborate plans he was putting in place, so I sent him money. He was to get us an apartment in Richmond, get a space for a laundromat and a preowned tyre business. Everything looked good, and I joyously bid Lagos, my city of birth, goodbye.

When Debayo and I got to the arrival hall of the expansive George Bush Intercontinental Airport, there was no sign of Adedeji, and his phone was switched off. I didn't worry; perhaps he was stuck somewhere or in traffic. However, I soon understood the import of the statement that we should never judge a man by what we knew of him years ago because people change, and most times, for the worse. Seconds turned to minutes and hours, and Adedeji was still unreachable. I remembered he gave me an address in Sugar Land. So, I ordered an Uber and went to the address. When I arrived at the house, I met a middle-aged Latino who gleefully announced that he had owned the property for over two decades and no Adedeji lived there. Adedeji had scammed me. He'd scammed me out of thirty thousand dollars I sent him to prepare things in advance for me. I sighed and thanked God that I had not given him all my money. I had about ten thousand dollars cash and five thousand dollars in my Bank of America account, which I opened during one of my frequent vacations in the US.

That evening, Debayo and I checked into a hotel. Around 10 pm, when Debayo was fast asleep, I remembered Adedeji's wife, Bukola, exchanging WhatsApp messages and calls with me when I had helped her deliver some parcels to her folks in Nigeria. I fished out my phone and called her, not knowing what to expect.

She answered at the first ring.

"Who is this?" She asked.

I explained myself, and she remembered me instantly, but there was hesitation in her voice that I would understand later.

"I've been trying to reach Adedeji all day."

She sighed. "Deji and I separated this past year, and from what I know, he is no longer in Houston."

Before I could ask any questions, she said, "Deji hasn't been sincere in his dealings with me and his clients. He runs a car title service company where he helps mainly Nigerians process licence plates and titles for their vehicles. He would take money from people and not do the jobs. I found out that most times he was in Nigeria, he was using clients' monies to purchase properties in his name, and he became notorious among the Nigerian community here for messing clients up. Soon, he got fewer jobs as Nigerians spread bad information about him. He had to refund cash to people who threatened him, but he was collecting money from some people and using it to settle others."

She paused again, and I remembered Adedeji's property in the Lekki Peninsula and her revelation about how they were acquired. I had followed him to two of the blocks of flats he had built in Sangotedo and Awoyaya. They were magnificent, with marble floors, plaster of Paris ceilings, chandeliers and more.

"On top of that, he was also womanising. He has a particular mistress he has been with for years, and I understand she is with him now. One year before he left, he began staying three nights here and two nights with her in a house just ten minutes away from our home."

My eyes were bloodshot by now. I thanked her, and as I was about to end the call, she asked, "I hope he hasn't taken money from you?" And the tears came like rain then as I broke down and told her everything. She calmed me down as best as she could.

"I'm sorry to hear this. Deji has been a disappointment. I regretted marrying him and filing for him to become an American, but for my children, I would have left him long ago. Whenever I told him to be straight in his deals, he would tell me I was too soft because I pitied his clients. He told me he had to kill his conscience because he had bills to pay. God will see you through."

We ended our conversation on that note, and with all she told me, my eyes stayed wide open till the early hours of the next day. I rained curses on Deji. I left out his generation because I didn't believe in visiting the father's sin on the son, especially knowing that he was also a disappointment to his wife and, by extension, his children.

"Dad."

I turned to see Debayo awake, rubbing his eyes to clear his vision.

"Why are you not sleeping?"

"I woke up to use the toilet," I lied.

"Let's go back to bed," I squeezed his shoulder gently and lay him beside me, our heads on different pillows.

On our third day in the hotel, I met Solomon, a Nigerian, who helped me get an apartment off Bissonnet Street by Kirkwood, famous for being home to thousands of Nigerian immigrants in Houston. He also helped me to get a security job at a store where shoplifters were known by their names, yet they roamed the streets free because the law did not consider them criminals. A minor misdemeanour is what America considers shoplifting unless the stolen items are worth less than a thousand dollars.

I quickly adjusted to my new normal. I donned my uniform, complete with a fez cap on which "Security" was embossed and stood by the door, powerless to stop the sea of shoplifters. Occasionally, I thought of what would have become of these shoplifters in Lagos.

On my free days, I did not rest. I did DoorDash delivery and also worked at an Amazon warehouse. With all I was raking in, Debayo and I managed pretty well. That was until COVID-19 came and held the world by the throat, threatening to take its breath. America closed its doors as deaths from the virus mounted in thousands every passing day. The store where I worked closed, the same with my other side jobs. As someone working under the table, I was not entitled to palliatives from the government. Only taxpayers were eligible.

My situation reminded me of how many people I once paid their rent, how many children's education I sponsored, how many people I set up businesses for, how many people I took out of poverty, and how many people I helped exchange hopelessness with hope. The more I remembered, the more pain I felt. So, I obeyed the voices in my head and cursed Adedeji, the evil man. I would have remained comfortably in the middle class if I had stayed in Nigeria with what I had after my business failed.

I became an insomniac. Thanks to the Redeemed Christian Church of God parish we attended, Debayo and I always had enough to eat. As the pandemic worsened, bills piled up, rent, electricity, gas and more. Electricity was the first to go. By then, I had been served an eviction notice. On the eve of our eviction, I chose the path of our ancestors, employing death to evade disgrace. I first thought of cutting my wrist with a knife, I thought of tying myself to the fan, and I thought of using poison. The poison option appealed more to me. I had no poison, but a Google search was all I needed to know that swallowing raw hydrogen peroxide could cause me internal bleeding and with internal bleeding, I was sure death would claim its prize.

Downing hydrogen peroxide, I succumbed to the insistent voices promising my torment's end. I didn't worry about Debayo. America would take care of him.

****

The next time I saw my son, my recovery had not been as fast as the doctor had predicted. Debayo's tear-streaked face greeted me as I turned to him. Seeing my twelve-year-old this way broke my heart. This boy, who had known both luxury and lack, wrapped his arms around me and said he was sorry.

The doctor's entrance, the one with the Nigerian accent, interrupted us. His lab coat was sparkling clean. Two pens, I suspected of different colours, peeped from the upper right side of the coat. His hair was protected with a cap, his face with a mask, and his hands with gloves. His fair complexion shone like well-moisturised skin. He had no wristwatch on.

Something about his face placed Nadia in my consciousness. My late wife had eager eyes, the type that made her ever noticeable. Dark, plumpy and athletic, Nadia was the source of my wealth. She led me to the two major clients who changed my fortunes. When she passed away, I passed away too. But I had our son to look after. Indeed, she kept appearing to me night after night, crying for me to put myself in order. She never let me be until, like River Nun, I answered her summons to make Debayo the centre of my world. I did not consider remarriage but instead had several very casual sexual relationships. None of the relationships lasted more than a year. I was forthright with every woman I dated and treated them well. I was also discreet as my son and businesses were off limit. My son did not need a new mother. I was his father and mother. My business did not need a confidante, I had well-trained people for that.

Dr Dejonwo's "How y'all doing?" brought me back to the present. I just shook my head and continued studying this clean-shaven man who had led the team that wrestled me from death. I wondered what his story was, who his parents were, how he ended up in America.

"You should be ready to return home soon."

I looked at Debayo, and tears began to well up again.

"No need to cry, Sir. Your pastor has told me everything. You're covered. We'll sort everything out when you're discharged."

He was out of the room before I could ask for details.

****

I didn't see Dr Dejonwo again until after I was discharged. He'd sent a car for us at the hospital, which took us to his white mansion in Cypress, near the store where I was a security guard. As we drove to the house, I noticed that Walmart, MacDonalds, Walgreens, Jack in the Box, Family Dollar, Dollar General and other businesses were closed, and the road was empty. Also missing were the regular long queues of parents' vehicles at the daycare centres and schools.

His house was on a street where every home had a tree in front and the US flag flying from the roofs. The trees gave the area a greenish shade. When we exited the car into the expansive compound, he smiled. I would find out later that the compound had a swimming pool and multipurpose pitch.

"Welcome home," Dr Dejonwo said as he led us to his living room.

"You must be tired. Let me show you to your rooms."

The living room TV was on CNN, reporting the latest death figures. Over one hundred thousand people had died in New York alone. The scroll bar on the channel showed that Saudi Arabia was not allowing pilgrimages from outside the kingdom that year. Israel had told Jerusalem pilgrimages to stay in their homes, workers were furloughed, and the Booker Prize presentation was going digital. Airlines had cancelled tickets, and international airports were ghost cities. The human race was on a forced break.

"I know you have questions, but you should rest first." He took us to an adjoining apartment with two rooms, a kitchen and a sitting room. "This is your place. You can stay here while we are working things out for you."

At that stage, I broke down—big time. The look on Debayo's face was one of surprise mixed with fear.

"Your dad is okay," Dr Dejonwo said, patting Debayo's back. "These are happy tears. Tears of joy."

"Thank you. Thank you," I said.

He just smiled and said: "The fridge is fully stocked. The kitchen has everything you need. Feel at home."

That night in the home of the man I later found out was from the famous Dejonwo family of Epe was dreamy. I slipped in and out of dreams with Nadia just smiling like she'd just won a jackpot. In one of the dreams, Dr Dejonwo's face and Nadia's kept interchanging, and at some point, she said, "You are sorted."

****

The lockdown meant our options were limited. Day in and day out, we watched TV, read books and generally lazed about the house. The news was all sad, and the number of the dead kept rising. Economies were collapsing, vaccine development was taking longer than the public expected and things were falling apart.

One of those lazy days, one month into our stay with Dr Dejonwo, I received a phone call. The caller was coughing as I answered the phone. I couldn't tell who it was from his weak hello.

"It's Deji," he finally managed to clear my curiosity.

He sounded nothing like the man who had tried to destroy me.

"Which Deji?" I asked, pretending as if I had not recognised his voice.

"Your friend."

I could hear his accent, and then he started coughing severely. Anger wanted me to end the call. I could hear someone telling him to leave the conversation until he was strong, but he replied that he had no such luxury of time.

Through coughs and sneezes, he told me how he fell sick a few weeks earlier and tested positive for COVID-19, with underlying conditions, such as high blood pressure and high cholesterol, had made recovery difficult. He was afraid for his life, as he had seen many people die in the hospital's isolation ward in New York, where he fled and regretted what he did to me.

As he spoke, I felt the curse I laid on him worked. I did not pity him. In my native Yoruba, the right response to his condition is to say God has caught him. But when he asked for my forgiveness, I couldn't say no, especially when he kept saying he doubted he would survive because he was worse every day.

He called me back two days later, sounding upbeat, barely coughing and sneezing. So, even before he said it, I knew he was getting better. He told me he didn't achieve anything with the money stolen from me and even went to jail after his girlfriend claimed he assaulted her. A part of me was happy he had seen hell. Now that he was getting better, I freely lampooned him, told him what a terrible human he was and made it clear that though I had forgiven him, I would only dine with him with a long spoon like the devil he was. I hung up after that.

Days later, his number would call me again. My first instinct was to ignore it, but I decided to answer.

"Hello," it was a female voice. "He died. The hospital called me this morning. He didn't remove my name as his next of kin and emergency contact."

It was Bukola. I extended my condolences. She hung up after that and left me feeling sorry that this friend turned something else became the first and only person I knew that the pandemic claimed.

Adedeji wasn't the only ghost from my past that resurrected. Even after losing my two big clients, I would still have been able to stay afloat with my third biggest client, but they terminated our services suddenly. This became clear to me six months into the pandemic when I received an email from Nkiruka requesting my number because she had important information to share with me.

Nkiruka was the lead strategist at A Plus Nigeria Plc, my third biggest client. She was also one of the women I had dated casually. I cut her off when she started pestering me to marry her. She accepted my decision and moved on, or so I thought. I sent her my number, eager to hear the information she had.

"Promise me you'll forgive me," was the next thing she said after we shared pleasantries and reminisced.

"Please," she pleaded when I was ruminating over what she had to say.

"Who am I not to forgive you? God has shown me mercy, so why should I be unforgiving?"

She then confessed that she was the one who got A Plus to terminate our services. In tears, she asked for forgiveness for allowing the devil to use her to wreck me. She was now born-again, a byproduct of the sober reflection the pandemic engendered.

"I forgive you," I told her as I disconnected the phone.

I cried afterwards, but a somewhat happy light shone on a dark episode of my life. I remembered another dream I had where Nadia told me everything would be clear to me and that everyone who wronged me were actors in a script to take me to a new height, one that would dwarf whatever I had ever achieved.

****

It has been three years now. The pandemic is over, and the world is fast recovering from its blows. Some may never get over it, but I have. Dr Dejonwo asked me to oversee the business side of his holdings when he learned I ran businesses in Nigeria.

We still live with this angel Debayo has dubbed the good doctor. We're still here only because he has not allowed us to leave. Whenever I try to raise the issue with him, he changes the topic. We're like his nuclear family. His marriage didn't produce any children, and his wife left years before our paths crossed.

Whenever I thank him for picking me up at my lowest, he shuts me up with facts about how his business is flourishing under my watch.

"You're my good luck charm. I would have lost a lot if I had not helped you when I did. You're a genius, and I thank you for helping to multiply my wealth," he says frequently, smiling.

Debayo is in high school. I am earning good money and saving for my son to go to any university of his choice, although I think he would most likely get a scholarship.

With his support, I have acquired two four-bed houses in Katy and Richmond and earn rent from them, and every day, I get closer to that new place Nadia promised.

The End.

Edited by Ibiso Graham-Douglas

Olukorede S. Yishau *is an award-winning and widely travelled journalist, novelist and short-story writer. His first novel,* In the Name of Our Father, *was nominated for the Nigeria Prize for Literature in 2021. He is also the author of a collection of short stories,* Vaults of Secrets. *His poems were published in an anthology of poetry Activists Poets. He holds a degree in Mass Communications and a professional diploma in Public Relations. Yishau was a fellow of a creative writing programme of the University of Iowa. He lives in Houston and is the United States Bureau Chief for The Nation Newspapers.*

God Abeg

Ibiso Graham-Douglas

God is punishing me.

This has been my constant thought for weeks as I watched my life spiral out of control, like a runaway tyre careening away from a vulcaniser, tumbling and rolling until it meets its inevitable fate in a ditch or a collision with a big trailer.

God is punishing me.

This can be the only reason for the chaotic mess my life has become. I mentioned this once to my sister, Biobele, when I arrived, but she silenced me by speaking to me about God's mercy. Mercy? What did mercy even mean to me? I felt no mercy, no deserving grace. I feel like I deserve condemnation, shame and ridicule.

My story did not start that way, though. It began in Eliozu, Port Harcourt. We lived a comfortable life. My dad, an oil worker, often away for weeks at a time, had worked hard to set up a business for my mother—a provision store that had grown into a bustling supermarket. In time, my mum outearned my dad, but they remained a loving and united couple who raised us, my two siblings and I, with love and the fear of God.

I was the last child with seven years between my brother Sodigi and me. Although my parents didn't spoil me, they were more lenient with me and gave me better opportunities in life than my sister and brother. I was the only one who went to a private secondary school. According to my parents, they no longer trusted the federal government colleges. Brereton International was one of the best then, so I went there. We planned that I would finish there and go to Covenant University in Ota, Ogun state, a relatively new private university. My parents, elders at church, had heard about this Pentecostal Christian university and were eager to have me study pharmacy or medicine.

The irony of life. To think that I could have solved my current predicament in an alternate reality.

"Come in," I answer to the knock at my door.

"Auntie Belema, Mummy said you should come and eat. Food is ready," my niece Soibi says as she opens the room door and peeps in.

"Thank you, I'm coming."

I join them a few minutes later, and her husband says the grace as I continue my introspection.

When they talk about the apple not falling far from the tree, it is my sister's life. She has built her life on the foundation of our own family. She is also married to an oil worker and runs several supermarkets in Port Harcourt. She and her husband, Uncle Bisi, are my parents but in a different generation. She is the pride and joy of the family. She and her husband are so Christian and kind that it is annoying. Why must they be so loving and forgiving? Why must they be so accommodating and caring to me after all I put my family through?

I called her a couple of weeks ago and asked if I could come and spend time with them, and with no questions asked, she agreed and was so excited. She called me several times to make sure I didn't change my mind and asked if there was anything special they could prepare for me.

She had some kind of PTSD from my disappearances and rejection in the past. Anyway, I turned up and have been here for about two weeks. No questions asked, no pressure about when I was leaving, and just generally minding her own business.

"This new virus is quite serious, and they've just announced that, like the rest of the world, we would lock down." Uncle Bisi says.

I zone out as they continue their usual family chatter, not thinking about the implications of the lockdown.

After dinner, I return to my room, where I have been ensconced since I came. As I contemplated whether to turn on my phone for the first time since I arrived in Port Harcourt, my mind went to my friend Anisa, the only person I felt I owed an update. She had been very helpful and supportive in the last few weeks.

I had left Lagos in a rush, and frankly, I was just tired of life and didn't have anywhere to go. God forbid that I had become one of those women people read about on social media whose backs were so pushed against the wall, they decided to jump off Third Mainland Bridge to end the chaos their lives had become.

My life had become chaotic. I do not know if the chaos started with Ikem or if it was after him, but I had so derailed from the plan my parents and I had and could not even read a map to take me back there.

****

By the time I had finished Brereton Secondary in 2011, my plans had changed slightly. I had convinced my parents that instead of going all the way to Ota to study, I should attend the new private university in Enugu. It was near Port Harcourt, I reasoned, a journey easy to make in a day. Also, I met the head of the medical department when they came to speak to final-year students at school. His name was Mr Patel, an Indian man, and he spoke highly of the department and the school and their plan to make us stars in medicine, dentistry and pharmacy. I was convinced.

I met Ikem during my very first week at school. He was two years ahead of me, part of the pioneer set of the university and seemed to know everyone and knew his way around, which helped me settle in. There was nothing sinister about him. He seemed like one of those guys that could have been easily overlooked in a room full of people. I met him at the Freshers' barbecue organised for the first-year students, and we hit it off immediately. He reminded me of my brother Sodigi, who had moved to Canada by this time. They had the same height, build and aura of confidence that was more self-assured than cocky. Somehow, this similarity made me feel comfortable with him. We hung out most days, and after a few weeks, he said he liked me and wanted me to be his girlfriend. I was naïve and innocent and really just liked him like a friend, and I told him so. I also told him that I was not ready to have a boyfriend. I remember his response that day.

"What do you mean by not ready?"

"I can't explain it," was my reply. "I think I'm too young to fall in love, and I really just want to focus on my studies."

The truth was that I didn't like Ikem like that. I liked someone else, Dubem, a boy in my class. We were both studying medicine and took the same courses. I always assumed that Ikem and I were just good friends as I had seen him with many different girls, and as much as I spent time with him, I didn't know much about him. He was like a brother to me.

Just as we were rounding up the first semester, Ikem invited me to his house for his birthday. He lived off campus as a year three student, sharing a flat with a friend. I had been there once on our way out when he stopped to collect his wallet he forgot. It was a Friday night, and he asked me to come early to help him prepare for the party. I got there around 6 pm with a cake for him, and that night, my life changed forever.

After that eventful night, I packed my things and left school. I went home to Port Harcourt and locked myself in my room for three days. Thankfully, my parents were not home, so I didn't have to explain why I had returned. My dad was away on the rig, and my mum had gone to Lagos to stock up for end-of-year hampers. I cried and cried, and Chisom, my friend whom I had told what happened, kept texting and calling and urging me to report him. But to whom?

I felt so bad, guilty and dirty, and I kept blaming myself. I trusted Ikem too easily and quickly. I mean, where did I know him from? I knew somehow it was my fault. I also felt bad because I didn't join any of the fellowships on campus. I went to church on Sunday, and that was it, so I felt like maybe if I had done that, I wouldn't have made myself so available to Ikem. I couldn't believe that after all the talks and advice my mum and sister had given me, and all the "girl talk" from my secondary school, I fell prey to Ikem's evil plan. I blamed myself for trusting the wrong person.

My parents were shocked to find me at home when they returned. My mum first and then my dad. They were worried about me, but I refused to tell them anything. I refused to say why I had left school and was refusing to go back but insisted they needed to change my school. My dad was upset and scolded me, but my mum kept pleading with me. When they realised I was not forthcoming, my parents called me into their room one evening, and my dad spoke. "Belema, we have tried to be good parents to you and be patient with you, but you won't tell us what happened in school. I have contacted your head of department, and there seems to be nothing wrong with your academics. It is my duty to train you as a father, and if you say it is Uniport you now want to attend, then it is Uniport you will go. Find out their admission process and let us know. But this would be the last chance you ever get from us."

****

Uniport was a different experience for me, and on one of the many occasions, "big guys in town" sent a bus to pick up girls in school for their party of highflyers in Old GRA, I went. I attended out of curiosity and boredom.

I remember Biokpo cajoling me that day, "Belema, come with us na, it would be fun! You never come for anything. Fine girl like you go dey waste your beauty. I don tell you say, you no need to do anything just carry this your raw beauty come."

I went with them to a party at this big house in Amadi Flats. I remember it was bright with so many chandeliers that reflected against the marble décor, making the place gleam. I sat in a corner observing when a man came and sat next to me. He introduced himself as Uncle Charlie and stayed with me the whole evening. Before we left, we exchanged numbers and became friends.

studied medicine or pharmacy as we had ... was now studying sociology, the easiest course to get into at that time. I could coast along and pass without really applying myself.

I graduated and worked my NYSC posting to Lagos. "Uncle" Charlie helped me. At this point, he was no longer Uncle Charlie but now Charlie, my Oga. Our relationship had evolved, and that's why I don't consider myself a runs girl. I never did runs. I just followed one big man, and that was it. By the time I entered Lagos, my game changed. I served in Charlie's friend's company because he wanted me available whenever he came to town and for trips.

He spoilt me silly with trips, gifts and money. I stopped asking my parents for things and got tired of explaining where I got things from and why I wasn't regularly home for weekends or holidays. In the time that I had known Charlie, he had been promoted twice and became a really big man. His wife and kids were abroad, so I was the de facto Lagos wife. We travelled together, and I stayed in an apartment he rented.

I had careened far away from my roots and my parent's plan, and with time, the distance between us widened. I was tired of their preaching, pleas and advice. I occasionally spoke to my mum, but my dad was so upset and disappointed that I stopped talking to him. My sister Biobele never gave up on me. She called me unfailingly every Sunday and would send prayers when I did not answer. I would reply Amen sometimes, and other times, nothing.

Two years ago, Charlie died on one of his visits to the UK to see his family. I still don't know what happened. I remember he was supposed to be away for two weeks, and usually, when he's with his family, we talk or text once a day.

After ten days of not hearing from him, I was frantic. He had not replied to any of my messages or answered my calls. His wife eventually sent a message from his number informing me of his death. I remembered the exact words of her message "Ashawo! You have killed my husband! Useless prostitute. You must be very happy. Call him in the grave."

That was how my life changed. Shortly after Charlie died, I found out I was pregnant. It would have been our fourth abortion, so I was determined to keep the baby. I went to his friend, my former boss, for help, but he also wanted a piece of me. I was depressed and sad and didn't really care for myself, which led to a late-term miscarriage that devastated me.

I tried to get a job but could not. I dated a few guys but couldn't continue the cycle of just hooking up with men. That was how I met Gbolahan, a well-connected politician in Lagos. He was nice to me and said he wanted to make me his girl after the second time we met. He said he'd pay my rent and open a shop for me, but I told him I wanted to be an actress. I was pretty, I had done a few background or waka pass roles in some Nollywood productions, but I wanted to enter acting fully. Gbolahan said he'd help me. I had heard that the standard Nollywood starter kit was skin lightening, a Brazilian Butt Lift, aka BBL, and a bit of liposuction.

A few people I knew had done it, and I had recommendations for clinics in Nigeria, Turkey and the Dominican Republic. I had found a company in Turkey and had decided to do it there because it was a direct flight, and the visas were quite easy to get. When I mentioned it to Gbolahan, he was excited and said he would pay for it. He first transferred five million naira to me. I decided to do the surgery before the injections. I felt I could tell people I had become lighter because I was unwell and had been indoors.

****

"Belema, can you talk?" With a quick knock, Biobele opens the door and enters.

"Yes." Dreading what she had to say.

"It's confirmed, they have announced lockdown for next week. Are you going to stay with us? Or would you go back to Lagos?"

"I'm not sure yet. Please can I confirm tomorrow?"

"Okay." She stands and makes to leave my room but stops and sits again. "Look, I don't want to pry, but I think I have tried for you. I have tried to be as accommodating and as loving as possible. But you give nothing in return. What exactly is going on in your life? You called me and asked if you could come over, and I agreed. Since you came, you have locked yourself in this room, crying. You only come out for meals just once a day, and you barely eat. What is going on? I respected your wishes and did not tell Mummy and Daddy you were around. You are acting just like you did before Uniport. And I know that something happened to you then, as I am sure it has happened to you now. Please tell me what is going on."

I started crying, soft, silent tears. Those kinds that flow from your eyes, too tired and too afraid to come with a sound. She is right, of course. Something happened. God is punishing me for what I had put my family through. God is punishing me for who I have become and what I have done to myself. God is punishing me for turning my back on Him. Biobele sees my tears and moves towards me as I stand and begin to remove my clothes.

"Belema! What have you done?! Oh, my God! Belema, what is this? What have you done? What happened?"

The questions poured from her mouth, but I had no words to explain or describe. Where do I even begin to tell the story? My life was such a mess. I was ashamed of how my life had turned out. The annoying thing is that I knew better. But I just couldn't do better. I was made for more but didn't know how to reach for more.

****

Gbolahan gave me the money for the surgery, and on second thoughts, after I received advice from some of my friends, I decided to have the surgery in Nigeria. The new virus that had exploded on the world scene was spreading, and a few countries in Europe had gone into localised lockdown, and it was rumoured that Turkey could join them. My friend Anisa had told me about a medispa her friend had used in Lekki that brought in surgeons from America, so I decided to go for a consultation, and I was sold. They had told me the Turkish people did not know how to craft BBL bodies properly and that their doctors from America were better equipped and understood African women's bodies. They had a few doctors in the country, and if I was interested, they could squeeze me in as the last surgery on this trip before they returned to America.

I thought it was a great idea. I figured I could use any extra money to launch myself—do a photo shoot and secure a good content creator for my social media. I even consulted with a media company and talent agency interested in working with me. Someone had also told me that with about one point five million naira, they could get me into Big

Brother house, which would be the best avenue to launch me into stardom. I had a new plan, and it was working.

No one advised me about possible complications from the surgery. They made me believe that the procedure was simple and that there would be no issues because I was a young woman. Scrape fat from my tummy and arm and pump it into my bum. When I woke up after the surgery, they said everything went well. They'd keep me in the ICU for a few hours, in the hospital for a few days, and then I could go home to heal. But I had to lie on my stomach for the first ten days.

After a few days back home, I couldn't breathe, and every time I took a deep breath, I had sharp pain like a knife in the left side of my chest. I thought it was because I had been lying on my left side. So, I figured I was good to begin to lie on my right side and back. Then the fever started, so I returned to the hospital.

"So, what did the hospital say?" Biobele asks. At this point, she started crying and repeatedly saying, What did you do? And Lord have mercy.

"I had to do a CT scan, and they found I had a pulmonary embolism and an infection."

I could not tell her what I actually went through. When I returned to the clinic, they said they could do nothing for me. Their doctors had all returned to America, and if I had a fever, I probably had an infection. They gave me antibiotics and said I'd feel better in a few days. I got worse. By now, I could barely move without feeling breathless, and the pain in the left side was constant. I was also running out of money. I had spent the money saved for the lightening injections, Big Brother and the photo shoot.

I finally called my friend Anisa, and she came and took me to a clinic in Oniru. Once they discovered that I could be ill as a complication of surgery, they said they couldn't help me and that I should return to where I had the surgery. I went back there, and they said they could do nothing.

By this time, I was so ill, I could barely move, eat or sleep. Gbolahan, who I had been telling I was recovering, I now had to tell him I was sick and no hospital would treat me. The conversation that day made me feel so ashamed.

"Come this girl, do you have bad luck or what? You know how many girls I don pay surgery for? Why your own go come get K-leg?"

In the end, he helped by sending me to a hospital in Gbagada. They discovered I had pulmonary embolism, which I was told is a blood clot in my lungs. This was causing the pain in my side and the breathless feeling. They kept telling me I was very lucky to be alive. The high fever was because I had an infection called cellulitis, which was causing pain in all the surgery-affected areas. I was hospitalised for two weeks and had to discharge myself because Gbolahan had only deposited one million naira for my treatment, and the money ran out. I called and called him, but he didn't answer or respond to my messages. After a few days, he blocked me. I emptied my bank account to continue the treatment until I had no more money left. I had to borrow to buy my ticket to Port Harcourt and went to Biobele's house.

****

"But how do you feel now?" Biobele asks.

"I'm still in pain. I am supposed to be on blood thinning medications for a few months. They said the blood clot should clear in time."

"I think we should go to the hospital. Your body looks swollen, and you have these scars on your bum, and what are these marks?" She comes close and is touching me and moving me this way and that.

"They call them surgery burns."

"We need to go to the hospital. No wonder you have been wearing baggy clothes and bubu since you came. You did not want me to see these."

"No, I did not. I hoped I would have healed some more by now, but that does not seem to be happening."

"Oh my God! I have to call Mummy and Daddy. I think they need to know."

At this, I go on my knees to beg her. "Sis, please don't tell them. Please. They'd be devastated. They are so disappointed in me. I feel so ashamed. Dad hasn't spoken to me in two years. Please, abeg, God is punishing me. I can't bear to face them."

She cuts me off. "Belema, you have handled this and your life by yourself enough. We'll take over from here until you get back on your feet. God is not punishing you. He is a merciful God. I thought you were joking when you said that the day you came."

At this, she starts making a call. "Mummy, good afternoon. I'm fine, yes, yes. Okay. No o. Are you busy? Please, can you come to my house?" Pause, "No o, no problem." A small laugh, "At all. Okay, thank you. See you soon."

Speaking to me, "She's on her way. You have nothing to fear or worry about. She'd be here soon. We've all been worried about you and praying for you. I can no longer hide you from them. They need to know you are around and have a medical situation."

She hugs me and leaves the room, saying she'll return shortly. I am panicking now. How do I face my parents? What do I tell them? Did I make a mistake by coming here? I was so deep in thought that I only heard them before they opened the door and there stood my mum. I hadn't seen her in almost four years. She had changed a bit—white hair and slimmer.

She screams as she sees me and starts crying, rushing towards me. She envelopes me in a very tight hug that elicits pain, and I groan.

"*Tie paka*? What is wrong? *E oju ibiya*? Are you okay?"

Nodding and crying, my sister comes to my rescue and explains, "Mummy, she has had complications from surgery and has to go back to the hospital."

"What?! What surgery? What happened?"

Biobele and I give each other the eye, not knowing what to say. I could tell that she did not want to out me. And so, I outed myself.

"Cosmetic surgery, Mummy. I tried to do a butt lift and remove some fat, but it did not go well."

"Oh my God!"

Biobele takes over and starts talking to my mum and assuring her that the most important thing is that I am alive and that God has answered their prayers. She was still talking when my dad barged in, opening the door unannounced. You could see the shock on his face when he saw me. He looked at me, turned away and left the room.

****

From then, everything went so fast. With the impending lockdown, Biobele took me to a Christian hospital in Mile 1. They knew the owner and felt I would be better cared for by them without judgment. Also, they had a chaplain who came daily to counsel and pray for me. He would sit in my room for a few minutes, ask if I had any prayer requests, share a bible passage and then pray for me. For the first few days, I sat silent and watched him talk about healing power and how God wants to bless and restore me.

Restore me to what? To what I never was? It was a long time since I turned my back on God as a student, so there was nothing to restore. One day, when he came and started talking about restoration, to shut him up, I told him I didn't need any restoration. My problems were bigger than restoration. I remember that day, he laughed and said, "Everybody needs restoration. We all need to be restored to God's original plan for our lives. Not our plans or anybody's plan for us, but God's plan."

That was how we started talking. I opened up and, for the first time, voiced the turmoil of my soul and how it all began.

That Friday evening many years ago, while I was helping Ikem set up for the barbecue, we started drinking and talking. He was drinking beer, and I, what I thought was Chapman, and that was the last thing I remembered until I woke up a few hours naked in bed with him. I was horrified. He had drugged me and raped me, and when I woke up alarmed, he laughed at me. Said I led him on and was asking for it. I quickly put on my clothes and fled his house. I was still reeling from that when someone sent me a link to a porn site the next day.

I didn't know that Ikem had recorded his sordid violation of me and uploaded it to a porn site, and was now sharing it with some of his friends on campus. The shame and embarrassment was just too much for me to take. I felt so filthy and violated that I ran home before it spread all over the school. I never felt the same after that day. A part of my soul was altered, especially because my violation and shame had been so public and ridiculed.

I also told him about Charlie and Gbolahan and my plans to take Nollywood by storm. I told him I had taken my family for granted and didn't know how to repair my relationships, especially with my dad. As I spoke to him, I realised how foolish I had been. There's something awakening about voicing your thoughts, especially to anonymous individuals without knowledge of your history. I found it cleansing and freeing.

I was in the hospital for two extra weeks, feeling better every day. When they discharged me, I went home to my parents, although I would have preferred Biobele's place. I dreaded being home with my dad. I was afraid of what he would say, but my mum assured me that she had spoken to him and he had forgiven me. When I went home, I went to his room and knelt, asking for forgiveness.

I couldn't go to Biobele's house because she and her family had been exposed to the virus and were in quarantine. Biobele, who had a pass to move around because of her supermarket, had become an expert on all the safeguards. She always had a mask on, sanitised so many times and took every precaution. But they had been advised by Uncle Bisi's office that someone he had been exposed to was sick from the virus, and so they were asking all the staff and their families to quarantine and be in touch if they felt unwell.

I tried to be there for her as she was for me, calling and texting every day to ensure she was okay. We talked and talked and grew closer, and as the seriousness of the virus dawned on me, I was determined to make up for the past years. She was more bored and restless than anything and was looking forward to the end of the mandatory two weeks quarantine so she could return to work.

That was why I was surprised when my mum woke me up in the middle of the night to tell me she had to go and be with the kids because Uncle Bisi had rushed Biobele to the hospital. She couldn't breathe.

"What? But I spoke to her today and yesterday, and she said she was okay but tired because she had been working late on her computer."

"Well, Bisi just called, and I told them I'd go to the house and stay with the children until they return."

"No, Mummy, let me go instead."

"Ah! No o, Belema. With all the medications you are on, we don't want to expose you."

"But what about you?"

"I'd be alright, don't worry."

And so, my mum went to Biobele's house and stayed there, calling in the morning to give an update. They were not back from the hospital, and Uncle Bisi wasn't answering his phone.

"Yes, I know. I have tried to call him several times."

"Okay, how are you?"

"I'm okay, Mummy. Are you sure I shouldn't come and help with the kids?"

She assured me they were okay. Later that night, she returned home sad. Uncle Bisi had returned home alone, explaining that Biobele had tested positive for COVID-19 and had been put in the isolation centre. He had tested negative and was sent home. No one could be with her. We could only take things the next day to make her feel comfortable. Her oxygen, treatment and drugs were covered by Uncle Bisi's company's health insurance, but she still had to be in the government isolation centre.

Early the next morning, my mum left with pillows, blankets, sheets, drinks and provisions. They wouldn't let her see her but took the things for Biobele. Through one of her old schoolmates, Mum reached a nurse who was in charge who now advised her on what we could do.

They said Biobele was seriously ill and on oxygen. They didn't know how it would go and advised that we pray for a miracle and God's intervention.

"What do you mean by they don't know how it would go?"

"My dear daughter, they have told us to pray for the best but prepare for the worst."

"Mummy, I don't understand. Prepare for the worst like how?"

"It means she could die."

"Who could die? I don't understand."

"Belema," my mum calls my name very softly. I look at her as she continues, "The prognosis for your sister is not good, but there is nothing God cannot do. They need to tell us the truth to prepare us for any eventuality. But don't worry, we are praying. God will show us mercy and help us."

I couldn't believe what I was hearing. Biobele, die. That could not happen. Not when things were finally so great between us. I was in a daze. I left my mum in the living room, went to my room and did what I had not done in a long time.

I knelt and began to pray. I was overwhelmed by the fear of losing Biobele. I started crying and begging God. "God abeg. Abeg. I cannot lose my sister. She is my only sister. I cannot lose her. What would happen to her children? God abeg, pity me. Pity us. Take me instead. My life is useless here. Her life has been most useful. God abeg. Biobele cannot die. God abeg."

I continue to pray as I hear my parents start praise and worship in the living room, and I stand up and go to join them.

The End.

Ibiso Graham-Douglas *is a seasoned publisher and book industry professional with over two decades of expertise. Her impact is evident across the literary landscape, with a portfolio of titles across various genres. As the founder of Paperworth Books, Ibiso firmly believes in the inherent richness of African narratives, considering them fundamentally universal and complete in their own right.*

Aproko

Michael Afenfia

"Someone can be kind and still lack empathy." The statement caught my attention. As I no fit turn well well look the woman wey dey talk the talk, sake of say e dey rude and inappropriate to put eye, ear or mouth where people wey you no sabi dey gist their own, na so I hold my glass of red wine tight. I come troway eye put for another corner. But while my eyes were fixed on the man playing the keyboard on one end of the expansive and nicely furnished living room hosting the intimate function I was attending, as if wetin the two elegantly dressed women wey sidon for the same table with me dey talk no concern me, my ears were tuned to their conversation.

Someone can be kind and still lack empathy. Oh boy! The thing wey the woman talk deep, e deep well well and e enter my body. The talk ginger me to sit up and pay attention to her and her friend or sister or whatever they are to each other. The woman talk make sense die, I no go lie. Besides her nuggets of wisdom, the other thing wey catch my attention na her accent, her very beautiful and forceful Nigerian accent.

"I say person fit dey good oh, but e no mean say dem fit put themselves for another person shoe," the woman repeated her earlier statement to her friend, but this time she spoke in pidgin English.

"But how that one fit dey possible?" Her companion asked.

The question wey the second woman ask na the same question wey dey my mind sef. How person wey kind no go get empathy? How that one take dey possible sef? I been think say the two dey go hand in hand as I reason am for my mind.

Honestly, the talk deep oh. I couldn't wait to hear what Madam Philosopher had to say to that, so I stayed quiet and continued listening, hoping they wouldn't notice that I could be eavesdropping on them. Because of the interest wey I get for their tori, I didn't want them to change the topic or move their conversation to another table wey I no go fit hear wetin dem dey talk again.

"Because person fit do kind or nice things—dem fit help old woman crossroad, visit somebody when sick for hospital, donate to charity or help somebody shovel snow from their driveway. Person fit help a complete stranger change tire for their motor, buy cloth for dem pastor or dash land wey him get for Banana Island to Church kpa kpa—all that one na just kindness and kindness no be everything. Empathy na him important pass."

Madam Philosopher reply no disappoint me, but I still wanted her to elaborate. I wanted her to say more. As if say she be mind reader, na so the second woman come ask the question wey dey my mind.

"Sho! Empathy ke? Kindness na the koko na, wetin come pass that one? Person wey kind be him brother's keeper na. As long as you dey help people wey dey in need you be good person for my books oh. For me, nothing pass that one. Person wey good, don good finish. Abi, how you see am or am I missing something here?"

"My sister, I no argue with you oh, but person fit even give another person money to pay him hospital bill or house rent or pay another person pikin school fees, all that one na wetin person wey kind go do. The truth be say, after dem don do all that one finish, dem fit still no get empathy. Person wey kind still fit no sabi how to put himself for another person shoe or try to feel how another person dey feel or even imagine or understand how their action or attitude go affect another person. That na wetin I dey try talk. I hope say you dey understand wetin I dey talk so?"

"My sister, I dey try reason wetin you talk so. Anyway, e be like say na true you talk sha." The second lady conceded.

From my assessment of this second lady, she be like person wey another person go fit to convince without plenty argument or grammar. Was she gullible or simply poking so she could hear more?

"For many years, me sef been dey think like you, but being an immigrant to Canada has changed me. Me, I don learn many things from my job and studying people so tay my eye tear open by force." This was still the first lady talking.

"Ha! I no fit believe say this man just go like that sha. The person wey talk say good people no dey last no lie, I swear. Everybody wey dey this town know say the man good. The last time wey I see am, e be like say na for Superstore abi na for Walmart sef. Him been dey buy groceries all by himself and the thing touch me. Remain small, I been wan ask am whether him sabi cook and whether I fit help am, but you know me—I no dey like put mouth for something wey no concern me. Na so I keep quiet waka pass the man. You sabi how I dey do my own things na?"

I smiled to myself. I didn't need to know her well to know she was lying.

All across the room, there were smartly dressed white people with drinks in their hands. There were also a few black people in the mix, with drinks in their hands. The white people were huddled in their own small groups of twos, threes and fours, and the blacks did the same. This separation, conscious or unconscious, made me wonder what it would take to get them to mingle and talk to each other.

Because of the many white people in the room, it made sense that the two women would converse in pidgin English. How my mama talk am again? If you no want make person understand wetin you dey talk, talk the talk for language wey dem no understand. Obviously, dem no want make the oyibo people wey dey the room understand the aproko wey dem dey do, and it makes perfect sense.

For my mind, me sef I dey wonder wetin all these oyibo people dey do for black man funeral, abi him no get Nigerian friends? The thing surprise, but as I no fit ask anybody I come kukuma say make I sidon jeje dey listen the tori wey the two women dey tori dey go.

I no go lie, I been no too get interest for wetin dem they talk at first, but as the gist begin enter philosophy and the man personal life and how e be say the man die a lonely man, the talk come sweet me well well.

If to say dem be people wey I sabi before, I for shook mouth for their talk, but as per say I no sabi dem and dem no sabi me, na so I come decide say, just like the woman wey talk last put am, make me sef mind my business. If nothing else, na person funeral we come, and I believe say in every culture all over the world, including my own, people must respect the dead.

No be something wey I dey like talk, but me sef I dey lonely for my house. I get wife and children oh, but I dey lonely most times. My wife Ifeoma, wey drag me come this burial by force, me and am don marry for eleven years now and I no go lie for una, e no easy oh. The thing no be beans. Me and Ifeoma, we love each other well well, I swear, but sometimes e be like say love no be everything. In fact, for this cat and rat phase wey we dey so, I no even think say the thing wey dey between us now na love again sef. It was love for like maybe four years, but everything after that na patience and tolerance.

Ifeoma and me, we get many things in common, I know, but because of our cultural differences, we argue about many things. If no be the kind of food wey we dey eat for house, na how to discipline the children. When we first meet and when we first marry, it sounded exciting hearing her speak her Igbo language all the time. I even learnt how to speak Igbo because of the love wey I get for my woman, but after some time, even that one sef come be like say I dey do too much.

These days, I can't stand it when she is on the phone or in conversation with her family and friends, and they just go on and on speaking Igbo and using words and expressions in ways that make it really difficult for me to understand the exact thing wey dem dey talk about. Sometimes e be like say dem dey do am deliberately to sell me or confuse me or something like that.

Don't get me wrong oh, I love her people and her culture, and language is an important part of culture, right? But sometimes, after a long day at work, I want to come home to something neutral, something we both understand—the sweet and simple English language that surrounded me growing up, the language I grew up speaking and was certain I would pass on to my children.

Ifeoma and I are different. I want to start my morning with a cup of tea or coffee, but Ifeoma doesn't like tea or coffee. Who on earth doesn't like tea or coffee? Ifeoma wants *agbo* in the morning and *zobo* at night. Abeg, na wetin I wan carry *agbo* and *zobo* do again?

Don't get me wrong. I bet there are many Igbo people out there who can't go a day without consuming the kind of beverages I enjoy, so I am not blaming her dislike for tea or coffee on her ethnicity or nationality. I just find it troubling. When we first started dating and even in the first few months of our marriage, I thought it was cute and adorable, but now, honestly, e get as e be.

Ifeoma too like village things, I swear. Every time *agbo, zobo, okpa, abacha, uba*. Every time na so so *ogini, ogini*, person go dey hear. From morning till night, man pikin no go hear another thing again for inside him own house. Haba! How person wey don live for Canada all these years no go like tea and coffee or associate with any kind of oyibo thing small? No be village person I go call that one like so? If I say in many ways, my wife no dey behave like civilised person, na lie I lie?

Knowing everything I know now about her, her likes and dislikes and her tendency to be quite Igbotic when she wanted to be, was marrying her a mistake? Should I have married someone else? Someone who wasn't always quick to remind me that she was Igbo and that I should deal with it.

Still, who I be to conclude say Ifeoma being passionate about her culture and not liking tea or coffee makes her a village person? Are people who don't drink tea or coffee considered uncivilised or incomplete in any way? I no think so. All I am saying is that sometimes, make people dey marry person wey be like them small, person wey like the same thing when them like and also share similar life experiences, passions and pleasures like them.

Drinking tea or coffee first thing in the morning is a tradition passed on from one generation to another in my family. It is a tradition I had hoped to pass on to my children, but Ifeoma stands in the way of its actualisation.

True, I don dey tire for her and all the things wey I give up for this marriage. I don dey over tire I no go lie. I don tire for everyday quarrel quarrel. Even before she drag me to drive her here because she no dey too like to drive for inside snow, we quarrel small.

The matter between me and her this time be say her younger brother wey dey live with us no wan shovel snow and she dey support am like say him be small pikin. Which kind of trouble be that one? Me, I no understand why na only me go dey shovel snow every time wey a grown man of twenty-one dey live with us for the same house. I go shovel snow for am, I go come still bring money to feed am. Abi na mumu I be?

Honestly, this her brother matter don tire me. Chidi matter don tire me, but that one na talk for another day.

****

I can never, for the life of me, understand why Ifeoma has to be responsible for the upkeep of her parents and siblings back in Nigeria to the detriment of our own home and the many bills we must pay monthly so we are not embarrassed by the bank for not being able to pay our mortgage or car loan or have our utilities cut off by service providers.

But what can I say? That is Ifeoma for you. What Ifeoma wants, Ifeoma gets, and na wetin I sign up for when I say na she I go marry out of all the women wey dey Canada.

My mama and papa been talk am oh. No be say dem no like Ifeoma or anything like that. I knew they liked her, but being my parents and knowing the kind of girls I had dated and introduced to them, coming home with Ifeoma Nwandike was a shocker to them.

After me and Miranda, my girlfriend that year been break up, na so I come jam Ifeoma for the automobile company wey me and her been dey work for Winnipeg. Ifeoma no too tall, but for woman, her height dey okay. Her skin, my god! Her skin dey smooth like correct Lindt & Sprungli chocolate. And as if the fine wey she fine for face no do, she come get thick long hair and her body na fire. Her smile dey mesmerising and she get sense join. In fact, Ifeoma na wetin dem dey call wife material, and I think any man would be lucky to have her.

The thing wey happen to me and her for Maxine Auto-Rush Dealership, na the one wey people wey dey write book dey describe as love at first sight. We fell in love hard and fast and put in our all because we wanted the relationship to work. Because she was different and nothing like the girls I had dated in the past, my parents were worried for me. They wanted to be sure I knew what I was doing and that I wasn't rushing into marriage with this new girl to get over and get at Miranda for cheating on me with the dark and handsome Jamaican pool boy in the hotel where she worked. To this day, Miranda insists that she didn't cheat on me. She said it wasn't sex but feelings. Her last words to me before moving out of our shared apartment were a prayer.

"Bill," I remember her saying, "I pray that one day you will feel it too."

I didn't say amen to her prayer. Maybe I should have. Some years ago, I ran into her at the airport, and she still insisted that she didn't cheat on me. Miranda said she fell in love with a black guy who was in love with her, too. The proof that the two things (cheating on someone versus falling in love with someone) were different was that she and this dude got married, moved to Calgary, had three kids, two dogs and a picket fence, and are still happy in the way happiness and happy endings are described in every fairy tale book I read as a child.

My parents been dey very concerned about me and my motive for proposing to Ifeoma and whether our marriage go stand the test of time. Not because of our cultural differences and other small small things wey dem been observe at the time, but I no send them and their I-too-know attitude sometimes when it comes to us, their children and the choices we make about our lives. I was in love with Ifeoma, and the love been shak me well well, I tell you. My people, una know wetin dem dey talk about love na? Love, it makes you do crazy things.

Do you know something else that makes you do crazy things? A global pandemic. A global pandemic of epic proportions and disastrous consequences wey confuse doctors and scientists all over the world. A pandemic that resulted in a complete worldwide lockdown wey be like say e no go ever end again.

Honestly ehn, the COVID-19 pandemic show us shege, I tell you. The thing almost make me kolo. Not even in a dream did I think I would witness or experience anything like it in my lifetime. I no expect am, and nothing wey I don do or see for this sweet life, wey sweet pass sugar so, prepare me for the scary and devastating impact of this strange respiratory sickness wey for more than two years kill people like fowl. COVID was not a respecter of race, nationality, ethnicity, class or gender. Nothing prepare the world for something like this wey make both the rich and poor people all over the world catch cold by force and nothing, absolutely nothing prepare me to dey house two-four-seven with my wife day-in and day-out for such a long time.

For high school that year, I been no too pay attention to biology or any of the sciences generally, but I still remember some of the things wey I learn about bacteria and viruses, and how dem dey spread and cause some of the bad bad sicknesses and diseases wey dey affect people, animals and plants.

From that time for school, I know say viruses dey harmful to our health and wellbeing oh, but wetin concern virus concern marriage and relationships? How virus take affect that one? My brothers and sisters, make una sidon first, make I give una correct gist. If person been tell me say virus go affect my marriage and nearly scatter my family, I for say the person don shayo, I swear down. But na the thing wey happen to us because of COVID and lockdown be that.

As if things never dey bad enough between Ifeoma and me before the pandemic, COVID-19 came and accelerated the tension in our home and brought things to a breaking point. It is a miracle we didn't snap. If I could describe how things between Ifeoma and I were pre-COVID, I would say it was touch-and-go. However, during COVID, it became touch-and-combust just like volcano and wetin cause am? I say sidon. I go give una gist.

Even though Ifeoma was always the volatile and unpredictable one in the marriage, the fire wey nearly consume our marriage and burn down our home, na me start am. Yes, na me and I talk am with my full chest. It was all my fault. Well, was it really my fault? Na me really cause am? Because as my people dey talk am, it takes two to tango and every coin get two sides, abi?

Like almost every other business, Ifeoma's small nail studio for downtown Winnipeg was closed because of the pandemic. The car dealership I worked for was also closed for the same reason. In fact, my own company been don even ask us to dey work from home before Premier Brian Pallister announced the plenty plenty restrictions on gatherings and businesses all over Manitoba aimed at stopping the spread of the virus and keeping people safe.

The whole of Winnipeg be like ghost town as per say people no fit comot for house again unless dem dey on essential duty for their working place or dem dey go buy groceries under very strict conditions like masking, social distancing and other small small things wey the government and health authorities impose on Canadians while scientists, university professors and pharmaceutical companies in different countries dey hustle to find the cure to the virus.

People wey sabi me go say I dey kind, but according to my two new friends across the table, is that everything? Did I do right by my woman, and are my actions towards her justified simply because my madam get her own wahala?

Sometimes you think you know someone until you have to stay with them in the same house for months and months and months on end. Come to think of it, if Ifeoma hadn't spent all her time during the lockdown watching Nigerian movies, ignoring me and barely spending time with our girls Angel and Ogonna, I wouldn't have discovered Twitter and Instagram. And if I hadn't discovered Twitter and Instagram, I for no slide down the slippery slope wey come carry me enter all the different different websites and dating apps wey nearly cause katakata for my marriage and show me a side of myself wey I no even know exist before.

So, while from morning till night Ifeoma balance for parlour dey watch Nollywood film and dey swallow eba and *ofe onugbu*, me I tanda for Tinder dey chat up different different women. If them swipe right me sef go swipe right and if them whine me, na so me sef go whine dem back. At first, I been no take the thing serious oh, it was all fun and games until I jam Nkay.

See that Nkay, ehn, the babe fine die, leave that thing, and her voice dey totori me for body. Nkay na the shy type so I no even sabi wetin carry her enter Tinder but she fine well well and when she tell me say she be dentist, the attraction and respect wey I get for her come multiply. Even then, it was all still fun and games and e still suppose to be fun and games until Ifeoma catch me one night dey do video call with my internet babe. I did not know that the toilet door was unlocked, and when Ifeoma burst enter the bathroom, na so all hell broke loose. Shame no go let me talk wetin me and the woman been dey do for phone, so make we leave that one there. The thing wey I go talk here be say Ifeoma para well well, *kpom kwem*.

"You see your life? Even if you want to cheat on me, why be say na with another Igbo woman, why? I'm upset, Bill, I am very upset with you right now. So, you search the whole Canada you no see another woman follow, na the one wey be Igbo like me enter your eye, abi?"

I told her Nkay wasn't in Canada.

"That makes it even worse, Bill," Ifeoma yelled at me. "You wan tell me say out all the women wey God create for this world—Australia, Germany, India, China, Ethiopia, everywhere, none of them enter your eye na another Igbo woman like me you come dey sleep with? Why you go do me this kain thing, Bill? Why?"

Even after I tell her say Nkay na just online hookup and nothing more, and say everything when we dey do with each other na on top phone e start and end, Ifeoma still no gree believe me oh.

"Bill you wicked. You be wicked man. Why will you cheat on me? Why would you do something like this to me at a time when it feels like the world is ending and all we have is each other? I know I can be much sometimes oh, Bill, but I can never ever cheat on you online or offline. I will never do it, I no fit, and if I ever do am, make God punish me."

Throughout the lockdown na so the woman no let me hear word again oh. So tay even the children come dey ask us whether me and their mother still love each other and whether we go divorce after the pandemic. For the sake of peace and tranquillity in our home and of say make we survive the pandemic, I deleted the app and broke things up with Nkay, but did it draw us closer? No. Did Ifeoma continue with her *agbo* and *zobo*? Yes.

It has been months since that incident and although things in the country are starting to get back to normal now wey the sickness don almost finish and the government don comot all the COVID restrictions, I no fit talk say na the same thing for my house. My wife and I are still fighting and if it isn't one thing it's another.

****

Anyway, back to Ifeoma and the funeral. Even now sef, I still dey vex small because before we leave house, she been tell me say we no go stay long for this place because she sef no dey like burial, but like play play, we done dey here pass one hour and for the last thirty minutes or so, I never take eye see my wife. Only God sabi where she enter and who she dey follow talk because my wife sef na another radio without battery.

Ifeoma too like gist, I know say she don dey do aproko for wherever she dey so. No be say I get anywhere wey I dey go or anything to do when we go back house oh, but e for better say I dey inside my own house dey watch hockey or baseball for television with beer and chips by my side than this one wey these women wey dey near me so wan take talk finish my ear.

As I think about them for my mind, na so one of them, no be the philosopher oh, but the listener, the one wey I feel say dey do aproko, tap me small for shoulder. As she take touch my body, e surprise me small but I no sure say she notice am because of the face mask when I take cover face.

"You don't want to eat anything?"

I must have been lost in my reflection about Ifeoma and our fading romance because I didn't realise that an announcement had been made about food and that we could all proceed to the buffet table.

"No, I'm good. Thank you though."

"It is jollof rice. You should try it. I know you will like it."

"I'm not really hungry," I said to her. I know say na lie I dey talk because na correct hunger wey dey hammer me as I dey there so but how I wan tell her say to chop for burial get as e dey do me for body? As I say I no go chop, na so the women leave me waka go collect full plate of rice, chicken, and salad.

"This rice sweet well well oh." Madam Listener said to Madam Philosopher.

"I tell you. I go collect the name of the caterer so I go use her for my pikin birthday next month."

"As you mention pikin so, e come make me remember something wey I hear some women dey discuss for kitchen when I go find water to drink before dem serve us food. The thing just remind me of wetin we dey talk about kindness and empathy since we sidon here."

"Wetin be dat?" The question was from Listener.

"I hear say the man pikin dem no come the burial." It was a whisper, but it was loud enough for me to hear her.

"Wow, the children wicked oh. How dem no go come their own papa burial ceremony?"

"No be the thing wey I dey tell you since be that? I sure say wherever those children dey, them go dey do good things and the people wey dey around them go like them well well and go dey call them kind. But shebi you see, dem no even show face for their own papa burial. Person wey get empathy no go do that kind thing." Madam Philosopher postulated. "Wherever those children dey now, I say make God punish dem."

"Amen."

"Make dem no see better."

"Amen."

Madam Philosopher wore a dark-coloured ankara dress that gave her a pious look, but I didn't think she was pious. A pious person wouldn't pray the kind of prayer she just prayed. She looked pious, but her mouth fit kill person.

"Na wa o. Even in death, him family still abandon am like dem abandon am when him dey alive."

"If na only him family abandon am before him die that one good na. I say the whole Nigerian community for this town abandon the man for years."

"But Nigerian people dey here today well well na." Madam Listener appeared younger. She too wore a dress made from the same dark ankara fabric as her friend, but her own asoebi looked more stylish and e tight for her body so tey all her breast and yansh be like say dem wan tear the cloth.

"People wey no visit am when him need them, na now dem wan come show solidarity abi brotherhood." She hissed.

"No be the thing wey I talk say empathy dey different from kindness."

"My sister no be lie you talk jor."

"But wetin the man do sef. Me I don hear so many stories I no even know which one be true and which one be lie."

"Rosemary, make I give you the real gist. The man been get money well well before oh. Three years after him land Canada, na so God bless am and him come get correct work for one big company here for Winnipeg as their accountant. I hear say some years after him get the work na so him sign one document without reading it. The thing wey him sign cost the company plenty money and land am for jail because the people come talk say na him commit the fraud. As this one dey happen, na so him wife say she dey carry their children go holiday for America. I tell you say this woman no come back oh. That was the last time the man saw his children. The woman, plus the children, I hear say none of them show today. I say dem no even dey here to pay their last respect to person wey don suffer well well for this life."

"Na wa. Amaka, I say bad people dey everywhere." Madam Listener did the god forbid sign with her right hand.

"That one sef small. As this thing happen to this man so, as per say him don go prison, na so all him Nigerian friends, people wey him help when things good for am, run from the man. Nobody visit am for prison. After he was released, him come friend one oyibo woman wey say she no go born pikin for am because she been don already get one pikin for another man."

"No wonder him sabi plenty oyibo people and na dem plenty pass for here."

"Na so. Anyway, after some years na so the woman sef say she no do again, say she don fall out of love with am and fall in love with another woman like her."

"Ewo! Which kain bad luck be that?"

"Just like that oh. As this woman leave am the man come try kill himself but the medicine wey him take no work. But according to wetin I hear, e be like say the thing affect something for him brain."

As she spoke, I wondered which she found sweeter, the taste of jollof rice in her mouth or the story she was telling to her friend.

"Wetin affect him brain, the medicine abi the depression?"

"E fit be the depression oh. You know say we Nigerians no dey too believe all these mental health things when oyibo people dey talk, especially when e be say na man dey suffer am."

"Yes oh, our belief be say man must dey strong. Dem no dey cry and dem no dey share the things wey dey worry them with other people. If man dey go through anything, no matter how serious the thing be, him suppose stand kakaraka carry am for chest. That is how God made men."

"Na heartbreak kill the man," Madam Philosopher concluded.

As dem dey talk dey go, na so I sight Ifeoma across the room. She stand with another woman wey I never see before. Na so I shout her name make she come rescue me from the wahala wey she put me.

"Ifeoma! Ifeoma!"

The way I take shout her name I know say she sef surprise. For her mind she go dey wonder which time I begin miss her like that. As she hear my voice, na so Ifeoma and the woman wey she been stand with waka come meet me for the table wey I dey.

"Baby, abeg no vex. I dey inside since oh," I no accept her apology, but na when we reach house we go discuss that one.

"This world na small world oh. I say because I be vice president for our Nigerian association make I attend the burial of our late member. I no even know say the man daughter na person wey I sabi. Worst of all, I been no even know say na COVID kill the man because of all the stories wey been dey fly around town about am and how him take die, until Nkiruka give me the full gist inside room just now."

"You sabi the pikin of the man wey die?" All the things wey Ifeoma talk be like news for my ear and I sure say she hear the surprise for my voice as I take ask am the question.

"I dey tell you eh Bill, na the same area for Enugu all of us grow up."

"Na lie," I said to my wife. "You mean say you sabi the man pikin?"

"See her here na." she pointed to the lady standing not far and coming to stand beside her.

"Nkiruka, meet my husband, Bill. Bill meet Nkiruka na her papa be the man wey die so."

"It's a pleasure to meet you." Thankfully, I still had my facemask on. Uncertain of her reaction, I stretched out my hands for a handshake and she extended hers to me, although with some hesitation. Being the gentleman I am, I totally understood her predicament, but I gave nothing away and neither did she. Or did she? Did my facemask help? Na my mask, maybe na my mask.

"Nwa nnem, ndo. Chukwu ga enye gi ike i mezie ihe mebiriemebi," I said to her in Igbo. "Abeg, make you take heart, you hear," I did my best to console her despite what was going through my head. I know I should have stopped at that, but I was curious to learn more and get some things off my chest.

"Na only you come your papa burial so?"

"No oh, me I don dey here since last week, but my two brothers came in yesterday from America."

"Oh okay. I hope say our Winnipeg cold never show una pepper oh?"

"E dey show me pepper oh, but wetin person go do? Anyway, we are only here for a few more days, and then it's back to London for me and my husband."

Her response came to me as a surprise, but fortunately, I was able to keep my composure in hopes that Ifeoma did not notice anything. Nkay had told me many things about herself but never told me she was married.

From the corner of my eyes, I noticed the two women near me freeze in shock. They heard everything the late man's daughter said. It probably wasn't planned, but the next thing I knew, they started coughing simultaneously.

If I am being honest, I don't think they were really coughing. I think they were choking on their sweet jollof rice and chicken. I can only imagine which was more shocking to them—the fact that the man whose funeral they were attending died of COVID, or that his children were there at the funeral or, best of all, that a blond-haired, green-eyed white guy in Winnipeg of all places could speak flawless pidgin English.

In solidarity with Listener and Philosopher, I cleared my throat, and even though my wife been dey look me with one kind dangerous corner eye, I no send because I know say no be only solidarity make me do am. It was an involuntary action to help me deal with my own discomfiture because as I stand near the gorgeous Nkiruka, the only thing wey dey my mind na how I go reinstall Tinder for my phone without letting Ifeoma find out.

The End.

Michael Afenfia *is a diversity, settlement and inclusion practitioner based in Saskatchewan, Canada. He is the author of the critically acclaimed novels:* When the Moon Caught Fire, A Street Called Lonely, Don't Die on Wednesday, The Mechanics of Yenagoa, Rain Can Never Know *and his latest,* Leave My Bones in Saskatoon. *Michael studied Law and Business Administration. When he is not writing or speaking to newcomers to Canada and locals about race relations and immigration, he mentors young creatives in Nigeria.*

Edited by Ibiso Graham-Douglas

Oxford Fellowship in Limbo

Obari Gomba

W<small>E</small> <small>TICKED THE CHECKLIST WITH CARE</small>
but the virus was ahead of us.
It had walked its way far up, spread
its fear and fevers and earned itself
a name on the Thames.

Over here, in my city named
after colonial Harcourt, I had set
my face on the kind beacon
of Oxford; it promised
more ways of knowing the world.

The plumes were ready on the hat,
the garb of honour was ready,
and the carpet was red
like the eyes of a dream.

All plans were frozen when the virus
soiled the fingers of my hosts;
the angst was incremental.
The virus seized the people's verve,
sapped their glamour and grit.

We made a pact on this: a guest
should not see a host in crisis;

a host should not see a guest
in crisis.

There were no flights to link two lands
in distress.

We cut our losses, and the fellowship
was committed into the uncertain
hands of the future.

Obari Gomba (PhD), *winner of both the Nigeria Prize for Literature and the PAWA Prize for African Poetry, is an Honorary Fellow in Writing of the University of Iowa (USA) and the Associate Dean of Humanities at the University of Port Harcourt (Nigeria). He has been the TORCH Global South Visiting Professor and Visiting Fellow at All Souls College, University of Oxford (UK). He is a two-time winner of the Best Literary Artiste Award and the First Prize for Drama of the English Association of the University of Nigeria, Nsukka. His works include* Guerrilla Post *(Winner of ANA Drama Prize),* For Every Homeland *(Winner of ANA Poetry Prize),* Thunder Protocol *(Winner of ANA Poetry Prize), among others.*

Edited by Ibiso Graham-Douglas

Heavy

Shehu Zock-Sock

In the soft glow of the child's nursery, she hummed the lullaby, "You are my sunshine, my only sunshine." Abruptly, a jarring noise shattered the peace, plunging her into a nightmarish frenzy, as menacing hands from nowhere reached for her. Startled, she awoke from the nightmare gasping for air, saved by her blaring alarm clock.

Breathless but relieved, she reached for her inhaler in the bedside drawer, taking deep breaths to calm herself. She was exhausted, physically and mentally. She sat up on her bed, frozen. She struggled to gather herself. The time was 6am. She walked to the bathroom and looked in the mirror but struggled to recognise herself—no beauty, just a tired woman with bags under her eyes. She was not motivated to care for herself. Her hair was messy, and her nails desperately needed a manicure. She opened the mirror cabinet filled with different medications, selected a bottle and opened it, pouring a few tablets into her open bowl-shaped palm and swallowing them. She then splashed the remaining water onto her face before performing her ablution ritual for the Fajr prayer.

Dr Samira Hassan was a beautiful, young, intelligent woman from Borno. She was the first of two children of the Late Gen Abdullahi Hassan and their widowed mother, Hajiya. Samira was a renowned professional in her career.

She was a compassionate and highly distinguished psychiatrist with a reputation for care. She had recently relocated from the United Kingdom to Kano, setting up a new clinic. Her practice thrived because there were very few private psychiatrists in Kano, and she was so compassionate that she treated both the influential and underprivileged, especially during the challenging COVID period. Driven by the necessity of social distancing, she effortlessly transitioned to remote consultations, ensuring her patients still received the support they required during the testing times. The transition had not been easy on her, but it underscored her commitment to the job and her steadfast dedication to alleviating the struggles of those she served.

Yet, behind the title of doctor and the office doors, a duality played out in Samira's life. By day, as she stepped into her workspace, a remarkable transformation occurred. She emerged as a cheerful, warm and composed leader. However, once the office doors closed, an almost instant metamorphosis occurred. The confident professional faded into a self-defeating, mentally drained and utterly exhausted person as if she harboured an inner struggle yearning for someone to share her burden with.

She unrolled her yoga mat by the window, the faint aroma of sandalwood incense mingling with the soft morning light peeking through the curtains. "Whoosah," she whispered repeatedly, seeking inner peace amidst her internal chaos, her fingers coaxing positivity as she prepared for the day ahead.

As she dressed for the day, she picked up her phone and saw the notifications and missed calls, notably from her mother, Hajiya. Despite the urge to respond immediately, she gathered her resolve and readied herself for another day at the office, though the unease lingered.

In her home office, at 7.30, the shrill ring of her phone pierced the quiet and recognising the voice, she sighed, "Good morning, Joy," it was her secretary, Joy Ijegwa. "How are you?".

"I'm doing well, ma. How about you?" Joy responded cheerfully.

"I'm fine as well, thank you. So, what's up? What's on the agenda today?" Samira inquired, anticipation in her tone. "And what about Aisha? How is she? Has her baby arrived yet?" Samira asked. Aisha is Joy's friend and co-worker on maternity leave.

"Yes, ma. She gave birth last night to a bouncing baby boy. We spoke this morning, and both of them are fine. Thank God."

"*Alhamdulillah!* That's great news. Please convey my regards to her. I'll call her later to congratulate her as well. *Gaskiya*, I'm happy for her. What appointments do I have today?"

"Well, ma, before that, your mother has been asking for you. She mentioned giving you several missed calls, and you have not called back," Joy relayed concernedly.

"Don't worry about that. I'll call her back later. She keeps calling at inconvenient times. What else?" Samira replied dismissively, her focus already shifting to the day ahead.

"Well, she asked for your home address, and I…" Joy cautiously added, sensing Samira's potential reaction.

In disbelief, Samira interjected, "You did what? Why?"

"She's your mother, ma. I didn't know how to refuse her request without making you look bad," Joy explained, trying to justify her action. Samira, with a mix of frustration and understanding, replied, "Okay, but... did she mention why she needed it or if she was planning to come over?"

"No, ma."

"Fine. What else?" Samira asked, trying to move past the situation.

"Well, you were scheduled for two sessions today—M Kelechi and Mrs Humphrey—but someone called in, sounding quite desperate to speak with you," Joy explained hesitantly.

"Okay, and who might that be? Didn't the person give a name?" Samira inquired, her curiosity piqued.

"He declined to give it. He insists on being anonymous," Joy explained.

"I hope this isn't one of those prank calls meant to waste my time! Was the number displayed?" Samira asked, her scepticism evident.

"Yes, ma. The number is showing, but you know how people can call with any number. But since your first session isn't until 9:30 am, I thought maybe you could take this before..." Joy suggested, trying to be helpful.

"Hmm, alright. Put the call through. Let's see if it's something serious," Samira decided, her demeanour shifting to a more professional one.

"Okay, ma," Joy responded, quickly connecting the call.

"Hello," she said, "Dr Samira speaking. Please, may I know who you are?" There was no response. "I understand that you refused to give your name to my assistant." Still no response. "Well, I'm here now. How can I help?"

The man nervously spoke, "I understand that you help people. I saw your ad on the internet."

"Yes, I do. I listen to people and try to help them understand how or why they feel and act the way they do, then I offer practical solutions."

"I don't think… I'm not sure you can help me," he said.

"Why not, Mr.…?" she paused, waiting for him to give his name, but he did not, so she continued. "Okay, can I call you Isaac? Since you don't want to give me your name."

"It's fine," he replied, his voice deep, croaked and hesitant as if he was unsure he should remain on the phone. "I have done something really terrible. Something I am ashamed of but don't regret."

"What did you do?" she asked, pulling out her notebook from her office drawer with a pen, ready to jot down notes.

"Something you'll instantly judge me for," Isaac muttered.

"Well," Samira responded, leaning forward, "I can't form an opinion until you tell me. Besides, it's not my place to judge anyone. I'm here to listen. Just talk, and don't worry about what I think for now."

"Hmm. I'll pretend I believe that," replied Isaac.

"Why pretend?" she asked. Samira could hear him pacing as he spoke. She could hear his voice in and out of his phone speaker, so some words were muffled while others clear. She could tell he was anxious.

"Because whether we like to admit it or not, people judge people. It's our human nature."

"I understand," Samira said, her tone calm. "But I am a psychiatrist. My job is to try to understand people, how they think, react, what influences them, so that I can render help and find ways to treat them."

"I'm not sick," Isaac insisted, his voice firm.

"Okay, you're not sick," Samira acknowledged, maintaining her composure. "But you called me because you wanted to talk, right? Well, I'm here, listening."

Isaac took a deep breath, the weight of his confession heavy. "I killed someone."

The room seemed to grow heavier with the gravity of Isaac's words. Samira took a moment to process, reminding herself of her role: to guide Isaac towards understanding and healing, regardless of the darkness that had veiled his past actions.

"Okay..." She responded, puzzled. "Was this an accident, an unintentional mishap, or what exactly?"

"No!" He admitted.

"This person must have really upset you," Samira observed, her voice gentle and understanding while simultaneously trying to discern his persona.

"It doesn't matter anymore," Isaac replied, a hint of resignation in his tone.

"If it didn't, I'm sure we wouldn't be having this conversation right now. What led to the unfortunate event?" Samira probed gently, coaxing Isaac to open up.

"Unfortunate?" Isaac chuckled. "The thing is, I don't necessarily wish I could undo what I did. To be honest, I don't regret it. And it's fine if that makes me a terrible person," Isaac confessed, grappling with his own conflicting emotions.

"I need to know so that we can figure out how to help you move forward," she said, trying to guide the conversation towards understanding.

"It wasn't an accident!" Isaac said.

"Okay?" Samira responded, absorbing this revelation and striving to maintain her composure.

"Now, do you still think you can help me?" Isaac asked, his voice tinged with desperation.

"I'm willing to try, but you need to want my help," Samira assured him.

"I called you, didn't I?" Isaac's words held a glimmer of hope, a flicker of desire for a path towards healing.

"Yes, you did. So tell me, what happened?" Samira redirected the conversation, aiming to understand him better.

"Let's just say I paid an old man's debt," Isaac replied.

"A debt? Whose debt? Who was he, and why was it so important to you that you did what you did?" Samira asked.

"That's a long story, and I don't want to bore you. I just wanted to speak to someone before I... I..."

"Wait a minute, Isaac," she interjected firmly, a hint of concern in her voice. "Slow down a bit. You said you killed someone as a debt to an old man. I need to understand why. Were you forced? How exactly did that come about, and who was it you killed?"

Isaac's silence turned deafening as if darkened with the weight of his memories. Samira sensed the haunting turmoil behind his silence, a silent plea for understanding entangled in remorse and moral conflict.

"I killed my mother!" Isaac finally admitted, the words heavy with pain and guilt.

"Sorry, you said who?" Samira couldn't hide her shock, her heart heavy with the weight of Isaac's revelation. But she knew she needed to remain determined to help him. Isaac's admission left her grappling for understanding, realising the depth of his struggle with his actions and their consequences, even in a different reality.

"Wait, I have a right to confidentiality, right? Some sort of privacy protection policy as your client, right?" Isaac stated, vulnerably seeking reassurance.

"Yes, you do. Whatever we discuss here is strictly confidential and cannot be shared with a third party. However, I have to try to understand and know you before I can work towards helping you. Why did you do it?"

Suddenly, the call disconnected. Samira tried to call him back but could not get through. She tried and tried but could not connect to his line. She started getting frustrated and agitated.

Her doorbell rang, startling her. She wondered who it was as they were still in lockdown. Movements were still restricted, and visitations forbidden. Walking to the front door from her office, she hesitated before opening it. To her surprise, a military man stood there with a basket of food supplies. She did not need to wonder who it was from. It was her mother. Touched by the unexpected kindness, Samira's heart softened. Gratitude flowed as she thanked the soldier and collected the basket. "Thank you very much, sir, *nagode*."

Samira marvelled at the depth of her mother's love. Despite her previous disregard for her attempts at contact, she still found a way to get the soldiers, the only ones permitted to move about during lockdown, to bring her food. While still anxiously trying to reconnect with Isaac, a call came in. Unknowingly, she answered, only to hear Hajiya on the line, her voice filled with concern and love.

"*Haba*, Samira. I've been trying to reach you for days, but you refused to answer. Half the time, the line is busy. I've even had to call your office number. Sometimes, I'm tempted to think you even blocked me. What's wrong, baby *na*? Is everything okay?"

Samira had not visited her family home in over a year, and the once vibrant communication with her family had now dwindled to a mere whisper. The turning point was the tragic passing of her nephew, Abdul. The family was grappling with the loss, and the rift it had created was palpable. Hajiya observed this unsettling change and felt a deep sense of concern. Their bond, once the cornerstone of their family, particularly between Samira and her sister, Mairo, had been the source of immense joy and promise for the family's future. However, the recent sorrowful events severely shook that foundation of confidence.

Months passed in a haze of unresolved emotions and unspoken words. Samira wrestled with her grief, struggling to find the strength to face her family. The memories of Abdul, so innocent and pure, seemed to hang in the air, a constant reminder of the fragility of life. Each day, the burden of grief pressed heavier on Samira's heart, leaving her struggling with herself.

Hajiya yearned to bridge the widening gap that seemed to separate her daughters. She understood the complexities of their grief, yet she longed for the warmth and closeness that once defined their family. She recalled the days when the laughter of the two sisters would fill their home, and she hoped to rekindle that joy once more.

"Hajiya, please stop exaggerating things. Nothing is wrong. I've just been very busy, and the lockdown has taken a toll, especially with the transition to working from home. Sometimes, I just need a break from phone calls," Samira reassured.

"Ehen, okay. So when are you coming home?" asked Hajiya, concerned.

"For...?" inquired Samira.

"To see us, *manna*. What else?" Hajiya pressed.

"Mummy, have you forgotten there's a pandemic with restrictions on movement?" Samira responded.

Hajiya persisted, "So what? Haven't they relaxed the lockdown a bit? Besides, you know those government rules don't apply to us. I'll call your uncle, General Magaji, and he'll arrange an escort to bring you to us here in Maiduguri."

"Ah, Mummy, I can't believe you just said that," Samira expressed disbelief.

"Said what? Ahah, *sebi* they've delivered the foodstuff I sent you?"

"Yes, ma," Samira replied.

"Ehen, So what's the problem?" Hajiya insisted.

"You know what, don't worry, Hajiya. I promise I'll come home soon. But for now, I have to get back to work. Please let's talk later," Samira assured.

"Okay... but before I go, promise me that you'll call Mairo!" Hajiya reminded.

"Yes, ma," replied Samira as she ended the call, but her phone started ringing again. She usually wouldn't pick up personal calls during work hours, but this was different. It was Habib.

Habib was a dear childhood friend turned boyfriend based in the UK, and although they hadn't seen each other since before lockdown, their relationship remained serious and steadfast.

"My darling."

With a gentle smile, Samira replied, "*Na'am*."

"How are you? I've missed you *fa*!" Habib exclaimed.

Samira chuckled, "Ehen... are you sure? With the way you sound, my battery should be drained by now from your calls and messages. But *inna na gani*?"

Habib chuckled, "Like I always say, I have too much pride and self-respect to let you see me finish."

They shared laughter and banter, their familiar rapport a comforting reminder of their lasting connection.

"I wish I had listened to you and planned my trip earlier before this whole global shutdown," Habib reflected. "At least by now, you would've been in my arms, safe and catered for, loved and protected."

Samira reassured, "But I'm protected even now. Who's coming to bother me?"

"You know what I mean," Habib replied with affection.

"Yes, I do, and I miss you too. But since your coconut head refused to come to Nigeria in time, we're both suffering the consequences," Samira teased.

"I know... by now, I should've officially come over to greet Hajiya with my father and uncles to make my intentions known," Habib sighed, regretting the missed opportunity.

"There's still time, alright? The restrictions are gradually being lifted, and before we know it, we'll return to normal with travel and everything. Then, I will see my big head again," Samira reassured, holding onto hope.

"Honestly, I've missed you so much. I can't even explain it," Habib confessed, his love for Samira evident in his voice. "I hope no one is there trying to 'help me' with you," he added playfully and protectively.

Samira retorted, "Have I ever seemed confused to you?"

"Better. That's the kind of confidence I love you for. I want our children to come out just like you. Kind, gentle, compassionate, intelligent, organised, confident. I don't even know how many kids I want yet," Habib shared his dreams of a future with Samira.

As he spoke about their future children, Samira's mood changed, a mix of interest and concern. "Habib *kenan, lepazzi*... are you sure? You're the type who will start talking about adding another wife in a year!"

Habib chuckled, "*Haba*, in a year? I can't do you like that! Why would you even think about a second or third wife? As long as possible, it'll be me, you and our little Ummi. Yes, that will be our baby girl's name when Allah blesses us."

"Already? What if it's a boy?" Samira challenged playfully.

"Then I'll think of something," Habib replied as they shared a heavy laugh, his voice filled with warmth and love. The future held dreams of togetherness and a family, a beacon of hope in their hearts.

Samira took a deep breath, mustering the courage to share her truth with Habib. "My love, look, I don't know how to say this, but I can't... I shouldn't hide it from you. I don't think I want to have children."

Habib was taken aback, unable to fathom what he was hearing. "What? No, come on, you're playing with me. Why would you even think something like that? Not even one child? Why?"

Her voice held a weight of certainty, "I don't think I'll make a good mother."

Habib struggled to understand, for in his eyes, Samira embodied all the qualities of a loving and caring mother. She was intelligent, kind, cautious, gentle and great with kids. He was confused, "Is it the fear of labour or something else? Do you have any health issues, or did something happen?"

"Nothing like that at all. It's just that I know myself, and it's not a phase. I don't want children."

Offering reassurances, Habib said, "Don't worry. Many people say the same thing until they hold their first child in their arms and realise it's all they ever really wanted. Don't worry, my love."

But Samira persisted, affirming that it wasn't a passing phase but a decision she had contemplated deeply. Confused and unsure how to respond, Habib ended the conversation, needing time to process what he had just heard.

Alone once more in her office, she rubbed two fingers gently on her temples, trying to ease the tension. "Whoosah," she murmured, with measured breaths in and out again to calm her racing thoughts. Tears welled up in her eyes, a torrent of emotions she tried to hold back, but they threatened to overflow as the weight of her confession settled in. The fear that she had just pushed away the one man she truly loved was almost suffocating. Uncontrollably, she cried, her tears tracing a salty path down her cheek, each droplet a testament to the ache in her heart. Doubt clouded her mind, questioning the decision she had made. Was it the right choice? Was she denying herself a chance at happiness, or was this painful route her only path to self-discovery?

As she traversed through her living room, her eyes fell upon an old family photo nestled amidst papers in her office. It was of her and her late father, and a longing shot through her. She missed him deeply—his wisdom and gentle nature were irreplaceable. He, an army general, had been the softest soul she'd ever known. Desperate for guidance without judgment, she pondered whom to turn to. Then she remembered that Isaac had hinted at an unimaginable decision. With trembling fingers, she dialled the number he called her with, and hope surged with anxiety as it rang.

"Hello," Isaac's deep and croaked voice came through. "Dr Samira, I'm sorry our call ended abruptly. I ran out of airtime... and well... I have no more money."

"Are you drinking, Isaac?" Samira asked, concerned.

"Yes, I am," releasing a loud, repulsive belch. "I would've invited you, but you don't drink... *haram*, right?" Isaac chuckled nervously.

"Drinking wouldn't help, Isaac, and certainly not this early in the day. Listen to me, please." Samira urged, gently steering the conversation back to the gravity of the situation.

"Are you sure? It seems to be helping me," Isaac replied.

"Okay, Isaac, let's talk. Let's start this again. What do you do?"

"I'm an artiste, or was an artiste. I never really went to school, but I learned how to draw, paint, carve wood and take photographs on the streets. You see, these streets were my university, and on it, I have worked my life to this point. I'm now an orphan; my father passed away a few years ago, and my mum, well, you know what happened to that one."

"So why did you do it?" Samira asked again, concerned, as she struggled to decipher his personality and looked for an angle to help him.

"I thought I'd be satisfied with killing her, but I'm not! I saw her dancing, laughing, cheering and even spraying money at the wedding. It was disgusting to see her there, like she even knew the meaning of the word 'love', wearing that silly shine-shine emerald green *gele*," Isaac recounted with disdain and sorrow. He chuckled bitterly, continuing, "She didn't recognise me, her little boy, the photographer taking her pictures." Another bitter chuckle followed. "You know, my daddy was good, always tried to do the right thing. Sadly, life punishes the good. That's what led to his tragic story. You see, my mother got pregnant and forced herself on my daddy, knowing that he would always try to do the right thing. She manipulated him into marrying her, only to eventually leave us for another man. A rich man whom she travelled abroad with after leaving me with the neighbours. She left and never looked back. You see, she left when she got tired of Daddy not having money for the life she wanted. I was eight years old."

"That must have been incredibly difficult," Samira said softly.

"It was tough. We struggled. He spent his life working, trying to care for me as best he could and rebuild his life. She hurt him even more than me, especially after he found out her secret years later. You see, he fell really ill, and the doctors said he needed a kidney. So I naturally tried to give him one of mine, but the blood test revealed my blood group as B positive. Daddy was shocked because he said 'he and Mummy' were definitely O and even bragged about it on the few occasions they weren't at each other's throats. So how could I have blood group B?" Isaac's pain and confusion were palpable as he unravelled the complex web of his past.

"You weren't his..." Samira said, her voice gentle, crumbling with empathy and compassion as she understood his bitterness.

"And that's what killed him! A broken heart. Anyway, that's all water under the bridge now. I'll see her in hell for all I care because that's where we're both going after this."

She could hear him take a big gulp of his drink and didn't want him to hang up, so she asked, "Do you want to kill yourself? Isaac, taking your own life won't make things better. I can hear your pain and remorse. You're a good man."

"How do you know? You don't know me!" he accused. His torment bubbled over. "Ever since..., all I see are women like her. First, on the streets and everywhere I went. Since lockdown, I have seen her in my dreams. Women like her everywhere—users, takers and gold diggers. It feels like no one cares about us anymore. It's all about what they can take from us or what we can give them. They sell their bodies and virtues for fame and status, while honest, hardworking people like us are dismissed as foolish, broke and useless. As a man, do you know I can be the most responsible, respectful and honest person, but no one values me if I lack money, no one values me? Doctor, I'm at the point where I want to end it all. If I don't, I fear I might harm others like her—the Instagram models, so-called influencers and fake actresses. It feels like I'd be doing everyone a favour by removing myself from the equation."

Samira tried to reassure him gently, "No, you won't. You are a good person. You wouldn't be affected like this if you were cold and unfeeling. We all face struggles, but healing and moving forward is possible."

"It's better if I'm not around anymore," Isaac muttered, defeated.

"Whose betterment is at stake here? Everyone carries their own scars and secrets," Samira acknowledged, her empathy reaching out. "You're stronger than you think. I can't fully grasp what you've been through, but it doesn't have to define you. We all need to unburden ourselves; I certainly know I do." Hesitating momentarily, the words she usually shared with clients now felt like advice to herself. "First, you need to try to forgive yourself. I know it's tough, but it's crucial. Second, confession. You need to own up to what you've done and seek forgiveness from those you've hurt deeply. Lastly, acceptance to face the consequences." Exasperated, "I wish I had your courage," Samira admitted, revealing her own vulnerability in the face of Isaac's resilience.

"Why would you need it? You didn't kill anyone in cold blood," Isaac reasoned, questioning her motive.

Her breathing became heavy as she contemplated something, her heart racing with each passing moment. "No, I didn't, but I... I..." Her fears became louder, her facade cracking. "I keep having this nightmare. I hold a baby, and people around me know what I've done. They reach for me, but they're just hands with no bodies. A year ago, I was holding my younger sister's baby in his nursery, singing, playing with and loving him. Then something went wrong! My phone rang, and while I tried to reach for it on the table, he wriggled and slipped from my arms. He fell on the floor headfirst. He died in that instant without so much as a sound. I was terrified. I didn't know what to say or how to tell the story of what had just happened, so I wrapped him up and put him back in the cot as if he were still sleeping, and I left. I'm such a terrible person."

Isaac listened as she poured her heart out. "No one knew?"

"No one! Except God and now you," Samira confessed, her voice trembling with guilt, sadness and a bit of relief and finally letting out a secret that had weighed her down for so long.

"You're not a bad person. You're just human—you made a terrible mistake, you're afraid. It's normal. Who am I to judge you?" Isaac said.

"I accidentally caused the death of my dear nephew," Samira choked on her words, tears flowing down her anguished face. "It wasn't intentional, I swear. But the burden of guilt has been crushing me, making it impossible to face my reflection."

Acknowledging the profound conflict within herself, Isaac whispered, "It seems we both need help."

"Yes, we do." At that moment, Samira, grappling with her torment, realised that healing was possible amidst the darkness that shrouded their lives. They discovered a glimmer of hope, a unique understanding only those touched by profound sorrow and indescribable guilt could comprehend.

****

As soon as lockdown restrictions were lifted, Samira travelled to Maiduguri to confront her past and admit the painful truth to her mother. "Mummy, I need to tell you something." Samira's voice wavered as she braced herself. "I know once I say it, you will never look at me the same way again. You might not want to see me ever again." She struggled to maintain eye contact, her heart pounding louder than her words. "But before I begin..." Samira lowered herself onto both knees, her voice cracking.

They were in the living room of her father's house and expecting Mairo and her husband Farouq to come and visit. Samira did not want to postpone the inevitable anymore and felt she owed it to herself and her family to tell the truth about Abdul. So that real healing could begin and absolve Mairo of any guilt about her son's death.

"Please, I need you to forgive me. I know you may never forget what I'm about to confess, but your forgiveness could help lighten this unbearable burden crushing my soul." Tears streamed down her face as she pleaded with Hajiya, who watched with confusion and growing anxiety.

"Please, Samira, get up," Hajiya urged, her voice filled with concern. "What could be so dreadful that you'd distance yourself from your family? Please, talk to me." Samira, tears glistening on her cheeks, mustered the strength to speak. "It's about Abdul."

"Which Abdul?" Hajiya's confusion lingered.

"Abdul. Your grandson, Mairo's baby, my nephew," Samira whispered, almost afraid to voice the words. "His death... it was my fault. I caused it." Her confession hung in the air, heavy with grief and guilt, as silence enveloped the room.

Hajiya began reciting Islamic prayers fervently, her voice echoing the intensity of Christian tongues, her eyes flashing red as she screamed, gripping her head tightly. "Samira, please tell me this isn't true. Tell me!" The confession hit Hajiya like a trailer, breaking her heart to pieces, tears streaming down her face, each drop weighed down by the enormity of the news, but after explaining the circumstances surrounding the untimely death and allowing Hajiya some time to process, she finally calmed down and spoke.

"Have you spoken to your sister?"

"Not yet. I'm not sure of how to tell her, but she needs to know." Samira confessed.

Hajiya smirked in response. "She's your sister. She won't kill you if that's what you're worried about.'"

"But it's her first and only child we're talking about," responded Samira.

"So how would you tell her?" Hajiya enquired.

"I was hoping you would help me before... she sees me."

Samira's guilt prevented her from facing her sister, fearing her reaction. She had distanced herself from them for this reason.

Mairo met them in that position, Samira kneeling by Hajiya's feet, but they heard them before they saw them. Their *as-salamu alaykum* could be heard from the front door.

"*Me ke faruwa?* Mairo asked once she observed their postures and demeanours.

Hajiya told her what had happened in soft, measured words, and her howl could be heard on the street as she repeatedly muttered, "*Wayoo... wayoo Allah na...*"

Everyone was crying. Samira, overwhelmed by remorse, pleaded for forgiveness, "Mairo, *ki ya fe ni. Ina rokonki da sunan Allah.* Please, please forgive me. Please..."

Mairo, stunned and seething with a mixture of hurt and disbelief, couldn't bring herself to respond. Farouq, torn between comforting his shattered wife and grappling with his shock, gently urged Samira to leave for the time being.

As Samira walked away, her heart felt heavy, uncertain whether she still held a place in her once beloved family. The weight of shared secrets bore down on her, yet she remembered her advice to clients: forgiving yourself is the starting point for healing. Slowly, tentatively, she had begun to heed her counsel, and her burden lightened as she embraced the hope that time might eventually usher in forgiveness and redemption, even if its glimmers hadn't yet materialised.

****

Samira could not recollect how she made it back to Kano from Maiduguri. She had been in a daze throughout the journey. It had been a few weeks, and she had only heard from her mother once and nothing from Mairo or Farouq. She sent them messages daily, insipid words that she knew made no difference, but she had to keep trying. As the grip of lockdown restrictions loosened and life returned to normal, she spent more time in her office in client sessions.

She had not heard from Isaac again but often thought of him. He stood at the precipice of ending his life, but she prayed he chose to embrace hope. He never called or visited to express gratitude or unveil the man concealed behind the troubled voice. Yet, an unforeseen connection blossomed, showing that even shattered souls could find solace in one another. She was thankful he forced her to confront her own guilt and every day, she tried to do the same with clients.

"As you recline, close your eyes, let go of any thoughts and breathe in and out. In and out.

Samira was guiding her client through a meditation exercise when the serenity was abruptly interrupted by the unexpected vibration of her phone on the table. Fumbling to stop the disruption and apologising profusely to her client, she checked who it was and saw a name she had been longing to hear from—Mairo.

Her heart skipped a beat, and she struggled to contain her excitement and hope while maintaining composure and reassuring her client. Whether Mairo's call held words of anger or forgiveness, Samira's emotions surged. The fact that she was calling her was all the hope she had fervently prayed for. Tears welled up in her eyes as she composed herself and calmly answered. "Hello...."

The End.

Shehu Zock-Sock *is the founder of Nerd Factory Entertainment. He orchestrates compelling narratives as a writer, breathes life into characters on stage and screen as an actor, and meticulously sculpts captivating stories as a director and producer. He graduated from Ahmadu Bello University Zaria with a theatre and performing arts degree in 2008. He lives in Kaduna with his wife and children.*

Edited by Ibiso Graham-Douglas

Original of the Species

Chimeka Garricks

"You are the lawyer for the girl who killed King Marine, abi?"

The warder asked this as he patted me down. The body search was part of the pre-entry protocol before I would be allowed into the Women's Wing of Port Harcourt Prison. We stood in a dingy, smelly, windowless office in the prison.

I chose my words carefully, "My client is imprisoned in connection with the death of Chief Opunabo King-Pedro."

The warder rose to his full height, as much as his hunched shoulders would allow, but he was still a head shorter as he squared up to me. I studied his close-cut, greying hair and the wrinkles carved deep into his leathery face. He breathed heavily and almost in my face. Ordinarily, I'd have stepped back because of COVID protocol and all, but I was too pig headed to back off from a stare down. Instead, I held my breath and prayed my face mask would protect me (I knew I was being silly). His facemask hung under his chin, and it reminded me of those Santa beard sets sold in traffic at Christmas. His eyes held his defiance.

"Oga," he began respectfully, "God punish you and your client."

The two other warders in the room—a chubby, middle-aged woman and a wiry, younger man—snickered.

I smiled because I found it funny. And because I understood, I asked, "Opus helped you some time ago, right?"

He didn't answer but glared at me with his rheumy eyes.

"Who be Opus?" the younger male warder asked.

"King Marine," I said.

Few used his full name—Opunabo King-Pedro. To most people, i.e., the public, he was King Marine (after the marine and oil servicing company he ran). To those who knew him, he was Opus. He was always Opus to me.

"King Marine paid his hospital bill one time," the female warder explained.

"I see," I said.

"You don't see anything." It was the old warder, still trying to stare me down.

"Oga Mukoro, King Marine was your friend?" the other male warder asked him.

Mukoro answered slowly, still without taking his eyes off me. "No, the man did not know me. Twelve years ago, I was in an accident at Emohua. I stayed in hospital, UPTH, for three months. Till all my money finish. I even start to owe hospital, and I can't pay again. One day, King Marine came and asked the hospital for the bill of all the people who can't pay. Some of these people, hospital have treat them, and they are well, but they can't go because they have not pay. King Marine pay for all of us. Not only me. Sixteen of us in male surgical ward. Seven in female surgical ward. Eleven in maternity ward. He did not know any of us, but he pay for everybody. Just like that."

That was just like Opus. Incredibly generous. Flashy and larger than life. He was equally famous for his partying and his random benevolence to strangers in need. School fees?

Bills? Rents? He paid them. There was even a legend that he paid the alleged debts of a widow whose late husband, a wastrel, had mortgaged their only house for a tiny fraction of its market value to get a loan from a rapacious money lender. The man turned up after the funeral, poised to take over the house because he was confident that compound interest had ballooned the original debt to an amount the widow could never repay, but he didn't reckon with Opus.

"Ah! King Marine na good man."

They all agreed on that. But I stayed silent because I knew better than to conflate generous with good, and I knew him better than they did.

The female warder watched me carefully as if she was reading my mind. For a moment, I had a silly hope—that my deadpan face, hidden behind my mask, would prevent her from reading my mind. It didn't work. She asked, "He was your friend, abi?"

It was a tricky question, but I answered truthfully. "We knew each other."

People who would've seen us together socially, calling each other Chairman or *imbēre*, brother, may have called it differently, but the fact was, Opus and I never considered ourselves friends. Acquaintances? Yes. Fellow guy-men? Sure? Fellow Asiama natives? Definitely. There was mutual respect, and I liked him—he was easy to like and naturally charming. But, because of our shared history with Layefa, we understood, without ever speaking about it, that it would be awkward for us to be friends.

"If he was your friend, why are you defending this girl who killed him?" she accused.

I considered pointing out that I never said Opus was my friend. But I remembered my rule about rarely explaining myself to strangers. So, I smiled and said, "Long story." I hoped my tone made it clear I wouldn't tell the story.

Thankfully, it was time to hand over my phone to Mukoro. I signed it off and hoped the conversation would end. The younger male warder searched my satchel, which held my laptop and Becky's file. The female warder opened the food delivery bag I had also come with. The aroma of jollof rice and fried chicken filled the office. "You bring food for your client?" she asked, incredulous.

"Yes."

"Hmm!" She counted as she took out the plastic food packs from the delivery bag. There were six food packs. She opened all six, and we stared at the steaming piles of smoky jollof garnished with onion rings, bay leaves, diced green beans and barely covered pepper-grilled chicken thighs. "Hmm! All this food for only prisoner?" She looked up at me and asked a philosophical question. "Is it good for prisoner to eat better than warder?"

I smiled because I was prepared. "Sometimes, it's good for prisoners and warders to enjoy the same things. Only one pack is for my client. I brought the rest for you officers..." I was familiar with the delicacy required in speech when offering bribes. So, I added, "...This is just to show my appreciation for the work you're doing and to encourage you to do more."

The younger warder licked his lips. The female warder beamed. She pointed to the food packs. "You mean, we take five and leave one for your client?"

I nodded.

"Is it only food that warder will eat? Even the Bible said man shall not live by bread alone." It was Mukoro. He was no longer glaring at me, and there was now a sly look on his face.

I slipped my hand into my pocket, pulled out an unsealed envelope and placed it on the table next to one of the food packs. I deliberately left the flap open so they could see it was stuffed with ten dollar bills. Their eyes popped. "Use this to buy water or wine, to wash down the bread."

Mukoro gave the widest beam, showing uneven teeth. "Ah! Miracle," he declared sagely as he slipped the envelope into his pocket. The female warder saluted me, "'Shun, Sah!"

I smiled but felt a sudden crushing wave of sadness because I remembered Opus.

Two things came to my mind. First, I remembered it was from him that I had learned it was best practice to tip or bribe in dollars instead of naira (even if the naira equivalent was sometimes more) if one could afford it. He always had wads of dollars, mainly small denominations—twos, fives and tens—from which he tipped waitstaff, doormen, porters and the like, and they almost always went crazy.

Then, I also remembered him because I felt he deserved better from Mukoro. He had probably spent hundreds of thousands of naira on the man's hospital bills, only for him to die, and the man desecrate his memory for a third share of two hundred dollars and five packs of jollof rice. Life, eh?

I waited for the moment to pass, then confirmed the value I'd get for my bribe. "I believe you will continue to treat my client well?"

"Yes, sir. No problem, sir. She's VIP now. She's the new first lady sef."

****

Becky paused with a spoonful of jollof rice midair and glanced at me. "Thank you for the food."

"You're welcome." I thought about it for a moment and decided to continue. "I think you should know it's actually from your father."

She stopped eating.

"What? You want to spit it out?" I raised an eyebrow. "What are you going to do about the meals sent to you every day for the last three months?"

She was quiet for a while. "I thought they were from you. They're from your restaurant."

"Yes, they're from my restaurants. But your father insisted on paying for them." I explained. "Look, when he told me you were here, I asked one of the managers of my restaurants to send you food every day. I understood the burden would have been too much for your mother. Your father found out after the second day and insisted on paying for the food. I refused to take the money, but he knows the account details of my restaurant, and he transferred the money there." I shrugged. "It'll be weird to fight a man who wants to take care of his child."

"Is it now he knows he has a child?"

In a different place, I'd have replied that her statement was a bit unfair and there was enough blame to go around in her parents' fractious relationship. But I didn't have the emotional bandwidth for that conversation. So, I just said, "They say, any time a man wakes up, that is his own morning." I realised I'd just quoted a proverb like some African elder and cringed at myself. Then, I remembered that at fifty-one to her twenty-one, I was probably ancient to her, even if I was officially middle-aged. So, I laughed at myself.

"What's funny?"

"You wouldn't understand."

I watched the other women prisoners mill in groups in the yard. Most of them were young, in their late teens to early twenties, so, at first glance, it looked like some rundown girls' hostel. I had visited this prison many times before, but this was my first time in the women's wing. It was marginally better than the men's wing, which was an exceptional hellhole, but they both had the same smell of decay, death and despondence. I hated visiting Nigerian prisons because every time I did, it sent me spiralling down a dark place for weeks afterwards. Till now, I'd been lucky, privileged even. I could afford to stay away from prisons and the practice of law if I wanted. I was a qualified lawyer, and I'd inherited my late father's law firm, which I grew into a thriving partnership so I could focus on my passion for running a chain of restaurants. I was still a named partner in the law firm, kept an office there, and had junior colleagues to do research and heavy lifting for me, and this gave me the luxury of picking and choosing the cases I wished to do. Typically, I did no more than six in a year. All pro bono. All for prison inmates awaiting trial but had been incarcerated for years, unlike Becky, who had only been imprisoned for four months. Becky's was my seventh case this year, and it was only because Tubo, her father, was the closest man I had to a brother.

"Speaking about your father, I also think you should know he came here with me."

"He did?"

I nodded.

"Where is he?"

"Outside in the car park, probably smoking a hundred cigarettes while waiting for me," I joked.

"Why didn't he come in?"

"Your father can't cope in hospitals, police stations, mortuaries and prisons. Also, he knows you don't want to see him."

"He's right."

I sighed softly "Carrying this grudge here is baggage you don't need. It's better to travel light in this place."

She looked away and absentmindedly drummed her fingers on a small Bible she had with her. I'd seen it earlier but preferred not to quip or tease her about it. I understood. Like in crashing planes, most people quickly found God in Nigerian prisons. After a long moment, she turned to me. "You don't understand what it was like."

"You're right. But I have some idea."

"From speaking to my parents?"

"A bit of that, but that's not all of it." I exhaled, "I know a bit of what it feels like because, like you, I was supposed to be the child of shame. I was also born by the outside woman of a big man. Back then, they called us bastards. Sound familiar?"

She nodded.

"You'll grow up hating your father, and the hate will comfort you like a blanket many times. But, other times, you'll understand you really hate-love him and that love, no matter how small it is, is damn impossible to kill. So, what will you do?" I shrugged. "You'll pray to God about it, and perhaps, you'll eat your food. That's what."

She chuckled.

"Eat your food, Becky," I said softly.

"I prefer Bekere now, please." She resumed eating.

I raised an eyebrow. "No more Becky?"

She grinned with a mouthful of food, "No more Becky for now."

I smiled because I understood.

It was Becky who was infamous, not Bekere. Named Bekere, everyone always shortened it to Becky. She became a wild child in her teens as Becky. She evolved into a baddie, a term I only discovered after I took on her case as Becky.

Then, there was the whole Becky and Hair saga. Late last year, 2020, she'd posted a picture on Snapchat, Instagram and Twitter. It was a typical thirst trap (another term I'd recently learned), with skimpy clothes, plenty of oiled skin and lots of cleavage. Three other things made the picture remarkable: her luxurious Afro, the glowing blunt at the corner of her pouty lips with its tiny wisp of smoke and the captions...
#BeckyWithTheGreatHair,#MyMilkshakeBringsYourManToMyDMs and #MsStealYourMan.

It's hard to understand why it went viral. Maybe it was because it happened just before COVID lockdowns eased, and many people still spent more time online. Or maybe it was because the picture had something for everyone. Some Yass Queened and Go Girled her, while others complained that she was glorifying cheating. The stoners posted weed emojis with the hashtag #LegaliseIt in support, while their opponents tagged the social media handles of the NDLEA, Nigeria's anti-drug agency. Because she is light-skinned, there were long threads, think pieces and heated arguments about colourism and privilege for days on Nigerian Twitter. When it was about to die down, a section of Black American Twitter found the picture, and noticed she was biracial, which led to another flurry of conversations about the politics of black women's hair. Then, because there was a rumour that the original Becky and good hair lyric in Beyonce's song referred to a white woman, someone from the Black American camp accused Becky of cultural insensitivity, something something proximity to whiteness, and posturing for the white gaze. This sparked a bitter Twitter war between some Nigerians and Black Americans, which lasted for about a week, and she fuelled the fire when she trolled the Black Americans by posting another picture of part of her face and lots of her hair with the caption #GoodHairDontCare.

Eventually, it all died down.

Then, early this year, the news broke that Opus, a.k.a. King Marine, had been found dead and alone in the presidential suite of a luxury hotel in Port Harcourt. Days later, the police announced that they had arrested the prime suspect, a girl who had visited him in the room and left shortly after that. They released the evidence, CCTV footage from the hotel, to the media. It eventually made its way to social media.

There were three clips, all taken by the camera in the corridor and spliced together in a single video to tell the story. The first, time-stamped at 3:18 pm, was of Opus shuffling into view down the corridor, swiping the key card and entering the suite. The second, at 3:30 pm, was of a girl with big hair sashaying down the corridor to the suite. She paused at the door and looked both ways down the empty corridor. The clip paused when she turned towards the camera, and it zoomed into her maskless face. When the clip resumed, she rapped on the door, which opened from the inside. She entered the suite, and the door shut behind her. In the final clip, at 3:46 pm, the door of the suite cracked open, and the girl, this time wearing a COVID facemask, poked her head out, looked furtively left and right as if making sure no one was in the corridor, then she slunk out of the suite, and tiptoed, hugging herself, down the corridor and out of view. The video ended with a thirty-second still of the girl's zoomed-in face from the second clip.

And everyone—those familiar with the viral saga months before and those who weren't familiar with it but could still see all her pictures and videos on her accounts—unanimously agreed that the girl in the video was definitely Becky With The Great Hair.

****

Tubo was exactly how I expected him to be. He smoked in the back seat of his car, with the windows wound down, the engine running and the air conditioning on. When I got close to him, he took a final drag and flicked the stub out the window to the ground.

I pointed at it. "How many?"

"Just seven." He smiled, "You know I'm trying to cut down."

I chuckled.

It was his dark joke from when he'd caught COVID in its early days last year. At the time, everyone who tested positive was bundled to a government-run isolation centre. All he suffered was a slight sore throat, so he had some freedom to roam the centre for walks and fresh air. No one knew how he smuggled cigarettes in, but when he was caught smoking in the bushes on one of his walks, he'd shrugged and told the furious doctors, "You know I'm trying to cut down."

"Don't smoke in my car sha."

He sighed, "Who wants to smoke in your rubbish car sef?"

I laughed because we both had the same model SUVs, and they were parked side by side. I collected my keys from my driver and instructed him to enter Tubo's car with Tubo's driver and MoPol. Tubo got into my car and instructed his driver to follow us in his car. Privacy secured, I started my car, and drove aggressively, as if I was fleeing the prison.

Tubo asked, "How's your goddaughter?"

"She's not my goddaughter." It was our running inside joke from when she was a child. "She's holding up. She wants to be called Bekere now, not Becky."

"Thank goodness. You know how I just managed to tolerate Bekere as her name. And I always hated her being called Becky."

"Really? Why?"

"I had two regrettable exes, both named Becky, remember?" He shook his head, and made a quick sign of the cross. "I have no luck with that name."

I knew he regretted that he didn't name her. He'd confided in me that if he could turn back time, he'd have named her Tamarapriye, God's gift. I also understood his unspoken superstition—if he'd named her, maybe her life would have turned out differently.

Years ago, he and Enemo, her mother, had an intense, chaotic, on-and-off affair. She said Tubo had promised to marry her; he said they'd generally spoken about getting married, but he'd made no commitments. I believed her. When she got pregnant, he accused her of trying to trap him and pointed out that she had another boyfriend. This part was true, but he'd always known about him, and it had never been an issue, just as she also knew about Grace, his other girlfriend and her rival. They had a big fight, and determined to prove that she didn't need him, she gave birth to the baby without telling him. As if to vindicate Enemo, the baby came out light-skinned biracial. Both Tubo and Enemo were biracial, with white fathers and black mothers, while her boyfriend was black. This seemed like proof, on first appearance, that the baby was Tubo's, but he refused to commit and requested a DNA test despite how much I tried to talk sense into him. His silly argument then was that Enemo and her boyfriend could make a biracial baby. Still keeping her pride, Enemo considered the DNA request an insult and refused. She named the baby Bekere, roughly meaning white woman, an obvious gloat after her vindication in the paternity dispute. She also gave Bekere her surname, an obvious pointer to the fact that she considered her fatherless.

The girl turned ten and into a spitting image of Tubo before he came to his senses. He tried to contact Enemo to apologise, make amends and contribute to the child's upkeep, but she rebuffed him. He would allege that Enemo's real anger was because he'd since married Grace by then. He spent a year pleading through intermediaries such as her family and me, but she didn't change her mind. We, the intermediaries, could see the child, but she never let Tubo meet her.

Frustrated, Tubo turned to court and filed a lawsuit to enforce his paternal rights. I refused to represent him. The case slogged through the High Court system for four years without progress. Due to the court's congestion, the first judge took about two and a half years to hear the case but died just before it was concluded. By the rules, the case had to be reassigned to another judge and start afresh. This took another year and a half till the second judge was elevated to the Court of Appeal, and the case was reassigned to a third one. By then, everyone was so battle-weary that I was able to negotiate a fragile truce. Tubo was to withdraw the lawsuit, make child-support payments, including back pay for all the previous years of her life, and in return, he'd get limited and unsupervised visitation rights. That was when he started calling her my goddaughter. Years later, I'd understand that he did this because that was how he mostly saw her in his mind, and he felt awkward calling her his daughter since they had yet to have a relationship.

"You know, I've never gotten through to your goddaughter. Somehow, life usually gets in the way."

"She's not my goddaughter."

By the time Tubo's visitation rights kicked off, the girl was a headstrong fourteen-year-old who'd started to rebel against her mother. She easily extended the rebellion to her stranger father as she sat silently through her meetings with him. Fed up, Enemo, with Tubo's consent since he was now paying the fees, shipped her off to an expensive boarding school in Abuja, hoping they'd straighten her out. Somehow, she got all twisted and strung out instead. One time, while in Abuja for some business, I dashed into Transcorp Hilton for a quick breakfast meeting but stopped short when I saw her at the buffet. I watched her load croissants and bacon onto her plate, then sit at a table with some middle-aged man with whom she'd obviously come down for breakfast. I quietly cancelled my meeting, apologised to my host, walked over, took her hand and led her out of the hotel without a word. I called her parents on our way to my hotel. I stayed with her in my hotel till later that afternoon when Enemo flew in on the first available flight from Port Harcourt. We returned her to her school that evening. They expelled her bright and early the next day, and we returned and took her home to Port Harcourt. She was sixteen. She managed to finish in another secondary school closer to home. By eighteen, she left home for university and somehow never returned, spending holidays with "friends" or in other cities.

"What I'm trying to say is, I fear I'll never get through to her."

"You're scared she'll be in prison for a long time?" I asked.

He nodded.

"If that happens, you must go there regularly and try to build a relationship with her there. You may not succeed, but you must go."

He exhaled and thought about it for a moment. "You'll come with me?"

"Sometimes, yes."

****

"I see you've come to try to take advantage of our friendship," Layefa said.

I grinned. "Yes."

She allowed herself a small smile in the circumstances. The circumstances were that, as Opus's widow, she was still in mourning. To many people, this meant she was expected to hide in their stately mansion in Old GRA, bereft, dishevelled and in black sackcloth. However, she sat in regal solemnity because she wasn't one to perform public grief and dressed in black chic because she'd never deglamorise herself no matter what life threw at her. The house was full of the usual throng of family and friends typical in the house of a recently deceased Nigerian big man pre-funeral. To get some privacy, she'd ushered me to an alcove in the giant living room, where we sat whispering on opposite matching sofas.

"If this feels awkward, and they ask, you can say I'm your lawyer."

She rolled those big eyes. "No one will believe you're my lawyer, Kaniye. Especially those who know you're the lawyer for the girl who killed my husband. But it doesn't matter anyway. I don't explain myself to anyone."

"C'mon. You know she didn't kill him."

Her jaw tightened. "What I know is irrelevant. Why are you here, Kaniye?"

"To pay my respects, give my condolences and pass on a message."

"Whatever you want to ask me, the answer is no."

"Let me ask first. I suggest you keep an open mind." I paused, "That way, it's easier for me to change it."

She smiled, and her eyes softened.

"I'm really sorry about Opus," I said.

"Thank you. But I don't believe you. Like everybody else, you probably think he deserved it." Then she muttered under her breath, "And maybe he did."

"First, I don't care what you believe." I shrugged, "I think Opus was flawed, just like everybody else. But I try not to conflate flawed with bad. Especially as I never knew him well enough." Then, I changed tack. "How're you holding up?"

She regarded me carefully. "I'm barely hanging on." Then she dropped her voice even lower, and the glint returned to her eye as if it never left. "But shh…, don't tell anyone."

"I won't."

I switched to why I came. "She didn't kill Opus. Yes, she was in the suite with him when he died: the CCTV clips say so, and she admitted this. But she didn't hurt him or cause his death. She always said he just collapsed. Nobody believed her. And I'll admit, I didn't believe her either. Until last week."

Fuelled by the euphoria of arresting Bekere and the public's reaction to the CCTV clips, the police, in their typical reckless way when they paraded Bekere before the press, made the expected noises about charging her with murder or manslaughter when the investigations were completed. This led to her being remanded at Port Harcourt Prison and denying the bail applications I made in court on her behalf. Eventually, it got to the time for a crucial part of the investigation—the autopsy. As was the process in these things, Tubo and I paid for a medical expert to attend and witness it on Bekere's behalf. A medical expert from Opus's family also witnessed the procedure.

"As you know, the toxicology report came out last week. The summary of the medical jargon? Accidental death due to MDMA toxicity. There were fatal levels of it in his body. If I remember the numbers correctly, there was 1.66mg of MDMA per litre in his blood, when anything above 0.1mg is considered fatal. MDMA is the party drug popularly called Ecstasy or Molly.

"Long story short, Opus took some Ecstasy sometime that day. Then, in the middle of his, erm, meeting with my client, he collapsed, went into cardiac arrest and died. She panicked, fled and was later arrested.

"In any other country, this is where the police will realise the evidence doesn't support either murder or manslaughter charges against my client, and they'll let her go. But this is Nigeria: our police are typically sociopaths. So, they now have an alternative theory. They say she induced him to take

Ecstasy. A twenty-one-year-old girl induced a fifty-six-year-old guy-man? I'm not one to judge, but we're talking about Opus here: he was partying hard before she was born. The truly mental thing is that there's no evidence for this theory—just vibes, as my kids will say. But, using this theory, the police are threatening to transfer the file to the NDLEA to prosecute her.

"I found out why the police are floating this theory. My sources in the police confided that they're under pressure from Opus's family to ensure that something is pinned on my client. By pressure, I include financial inducements." I sighed, "The police are also predictable in that they're happy to be persuaded by all sides."

Her face had since hardened, but I didn't care. "If the police transfer the file to the NDLEA, the worst thing that can happen to our side is we'll go through the irritation of a long trial while the girl remains in prison. As I said, there is no evidence against her, so she will be freed in the end, either at the trial or on appeal. It may take years, but it will happen.

"However, the outcomes will be different for your side. Or should I say, Opus's family's side? As I said, Opus partied hard for a long time. He also, how do I say this delicately? He embraced modern culture and technology and liked to record videos of himself and his female companions. Consensually, I must add. I just discovered that this was an open secret in the circles he rolled in. The worrying thing for your side is that I've managed to find two videos of Opus with two other girls. The sex isn't the interesting part of the videos. It's the fact that, somewhere in the middle of both videos, Opus popped some coloured pills. Now, I don't know what those pills are. They could be his medication or Viagra.

I'm willing to give him the benefit of the doubt, but the NDLEA, like most Nigerian security agencies, won't be so kind. They'll most likely believe it's Ecstasy and refuse to be convinced otherwise. You know why? Because they have the power to investigate the sources of income of drug users, and depending on how it goes, they can also go after their properties. Opus was a multi-millionaire, right? They'll want to eat all his bread or a big chunk of it. They'll investigate how he made his money. They'll disrupt his surviving businesses. They'll search all his houses, including this one, for drugs. They may even seal the houses while they investigate. And, of course, they may try to freeze all bank accounts linked to him while this happens. How will you and your kids cope? Oh, I forgot. The videos will also go public, and the court of public opinion will judge the matter. And I'll use the videos in her defence during her trial. It'll be a long and tortuous process for you, and you'll lose many things in the end.

    I unsteepled my fingers and leaned back. "As I said, I also came here to pass on a message. Do you understand my message, Layefa?"

    Her smile was tight. "I understand you just threatened me, Kaniye."

    I tsked and shook my head. "You misunderstood. I didn't threaten you. I made you a promise."

    I took a long moment before I spoke. My tone was conciliatory, my voice softer. "God knows, I liked Opus. But compared to this girl, he means nothing to me." I paused again. "This is where I shamelessly try to take advantage of our friendship, for old times' sake. The punishment for sleeping with your husband on the day he died cannot be unjust imprisonment. She's been in prison for months and has suffered enough. Call off your police thugs, Layefa. Let her go home. She's just twenty-one. You were twenty-one once, remember?"

From when she was twenty-one till sometime after her twenty-third birthday, Layefa and I were in love. Or we believed we were. When we met, I was a young, struggling lawyer, a year or two out of Law School. She was in her final year of university. We seemed perfect together—we made each other laugh easily, were emotionally compatible and shared a strong sexual chemistry. We were each other's first great loves. It was young love, high on wide-eyed dreams of a future together but blind to the realities of real life. One reality was that she was the first child of seven from a poor home with the clear expectation that she'd marry early and marry well to secure their tickets to better lives. The second reality was Opus, whom she met fortuitously just before her twenty-third birthday. He was ten years older and had been a millionaire for three years by then, and when he decided to throw her a surprise birthday party in his usual style of random generosity, it was the beginning of the end. I'd get jealous. We'd fight. We'd make up. But the cracks grew deeper. Eventually, we broke up officially three months later. He replaced me almost immediately. They got married just before her twenty-fourth birthday and spent that day in Monaco as part of their honeymoon resort-hopping itinerary on the French Riviera.

It would be easy to say it was the money that did it. But having met the suave Opus, seen his easy charm, laughed uproariously at his jokes (despite how much I needed to hate him), and observed him as the life of his life's party, I realised the truth—he was a better choice then, and she didn't stand a chance.

It took me three years to get over Layefa. It didn't help that during that time, we reconnected and had a brief, steamy affair. At first, despite the guilt, I felt I was getting one back at Opus. Until I realised, she was using me to get back at him after she discovered his affairs. My victory felt hollow, the guilt grew stronger, I regained my senses, and I ended things. But we remained friendly enough that I could invite her and Opus to my wedding years later. She came alone and watched Deola and me dance with an indecipherable look in her eye.

After a long while, Layefa took a deep breath. "Why are you fighting so much for this girl? Who is she?"

I didn't hesitate or think when I replied, "She's my goddaughter."

****

We rode in silence, both of us deep in thought.

Oddly, I had Opus on my mind—he'd been locked there since I woke that morning. I drove slowly, aimlessly at first, afraid to unnerve her. On Aggrey Road, I signalled to switch lanes, and uncharacteristically, a commercial bus slowed as if to allow me. Unsure, I glanced at the driver to confirm, and he flashed a thumbs-up. I returned the signal, and as I passed his bus, I espied a "Donated by King Marine Ltd." sticker on it. It was silly, but the moment felt serendipitous: as if, somehow, Opus had also given us a pass.

She sat low and huddled in the front passenger seat. She seemed smaller than I remembered. Younger too. Maybe it was because she wore her hair in long, thick cornrows. She couldn't stop shivering, but she shook her head when I asked if I should regulate or turn off the air conditioning. Eventually, I said, "There's a bag in the back seat with some new clothes and products for you. Your mother told us your sizes. We can order some more of what you want online later."

"Thank you so much." Her voice was thin and shaky.

"Your parents know you've been released. But I asked them not to come to the prison to pick you up because I figured you don't want them to see you yet, and you need some time."

She nodded. "I just need a place to shower and sleep until mid-morning tomorrow. Then, I'll see them, and…" Her words trailed off.

"You can do that at my house. Your parents want to see you as soon as possible, but I'll hold them off till noon tomorrow. Okay?"

"Yes, thank you." She fidgeted with the seatbelt. "After tomorrow, I'll find a place…"

I shook my head, "Don't. The room you'll stay in tonight, Deola and I decided to make it yours. So, see our house as your home. There'll always be food, Wi-Fi, uninterrupted power and, hopefully, peace. You can stay as long as you want. And if you go, no matter how far, you can always come back." I turned to glance at her. "Do you understand me, Bekere?"

She nodded vigorously and turned away to look out the window as we rolled towards home.

And I pretended I didn't see her flowing tears.

The End.

Chimeka Garricks *is a versatile writer and editor known for his captivating storytelling. He is the acclaimed author behind the collection of short stories,* A Broken People's Playlist, *and the* *compelling novel* Tomorrow Died Yesterday. *He counts literary greats such as Celeste Mohammed, Chuma Nwokolo and Cyprian Ekwensi among his favourite writers. He is currently immersed in crafting his next novel—although, as he playfully admits,* e get as e be.

Captured Moments

Michael W. Ndiomu

"But why do you have to go, Femi? And why today?" Hannatu asked as they drove to the airport. "Why not wait until we have some clarity about this disease?"

They were already on the Mobolaji Bank-Anthony Way leading to the domestic airport. Femi had insisted that Hannatu drive because he didn't want any delays with finding parking when they got there.

"I already explained that this is an opportunity to see the ministry's permanent secretary for that contract we are bidding on. You know how long I've been working on this and how many trips I've had to make already." Femi replied, getting a bit testy.

"But that is exactly why I'm worried. You've gone there several times already, three times this year alone, yet no approvals. It's always one thing or another. The permanent secretary you were close to has retired, so you have to start the process again with this new person."

"Is it now my fault that the other man was old and had to retire?"

"Femi, I'm not saying it's your fault! Why are you changing my words? I'm talking about the timing and everything happening in the country now. She turned to look at him, appealing to him with her eyes.

"Madam, face the road, na. Ah!" was his curt retort, not even bothering to look at her.

She turned to face the road, biting back her words.

The traffic opened up, and she accelerated, trying to get ahead before the commercial bus cut in front of her and blocked the road. The car spluttered, then picked up speed.

She had complained several times about the car, but Femi always reminded her about their current financial situation, promising to get a new car once the contract was approved.

She got to the airport in time for his flight and turned into the car park.

"No, no, don't bother going into the car park. Just drop me off." Femi said.

"Ah, ah! Let me park the car so I can follow you in and see you off after you get your boarding pass. We don't know how long you will be in Abuja on this trip." Hannatu responded.

"There's no need. It's not like it's my first time travelling by air."

"Haba, Femi. You know that's not what I mean. You know what, it's okay." She stopped talking and manoeuvred the car into a space between two cars in front of the terminal building. She parked the car and turned to Femi, who already had his hand on the door handle.

She reached out and touched his left arm, and he stopped.

"What is it now?" Femi asked.

"Ah ah, can't I hug and kiss my own husband goodbye again?"

"Madam, it's just Abuja I'm going to, not a transatlantic journey. I'll be back in a few days."

"Okay, no problem. Have a safe trip." She unlocked the doors so he could retrieve his carry-on suitcase from the back seat. "Do you have your facemask?"

"Yes, I do. I have extra masks and even gloves. Thank you." He said as he exited the vehicle and closed the back door. He stood to his full height and started walking towards the departure doors of the terminal building, and Hannatu was reminded of how attractive he was. Femi was tall, dark-skinned, fit and athletic. In his well-ironed dark green kaftan and hat, he could easily pass for a senator or the CEO of one of the numerous successful companies owned by powerful figures in Abuja.

When he got to the door of the building, he turned and waved. As the sunlight glinted off his glasses, his lips were slightly open in a small smile, and his white teeth peeked through, causing Hannatu's heart to flutter in her chest. She put her right hand over her left breast, and her body heaved with the memory of how manly his naked body was.

"Damn, this man is fine." She muttered to herself, smiling sheepishly. "And he's mine, my husband, my CEO… if only things were the way they used to be…"

"Madam, you wan sleep here? Dey go your way na, make we no arrest you." A security operative shouted at her to move on, bringing her out of her warm reverie. She quickly put the car in gear and drove off.

As Hannatu drove home, she started thinking of how ideal their married life used to be. Everything had been perfect. Her wants and desires were all fulfilled when she walked down the aisle with Femi, the love of her life. Their wedding and the honeymoon were a blast straight out of a fairytale. And when their daughter was born, Hannatu couldn't contain her joy. Femi spent every free minute with her. Not even his mother's mutterings about the male grandchild she wanted to carry before she died could dampen Femi's spirits. All this was before he founded his new company and had to pursue government contracts. Hannatu hoped that with this trip, he would be able to secure this contract that he had been after for so long, and maybe, hopefully, things would get back to the way they used to be between them.

****

The year was 2007, and Hannatu Kolawole was in her third year at the University of Lagos. She was a very shy, tall, lean girl with loose-fitting clothes. She had entered university relatively young and was quite naïve. Her mother had drummed into her the dangers of boys, so she religiously avoided parties on campus, visits to the boys' hostels or any of the sketchy social gatherings that other girls were so happy to attend. She had thus gotten to her third year without any romantic entanglements. Being the only child of a strict Christian family, she had lived a sheltered life. The untimely death of her father when she was ten only made her mother more protective of her. So, getting into the university, she focused on studying and graduating with a first-class degree.

That was until she met Femi Adewale.

She was running late for a lecture one Tuesday morning and waiting for a bus at the main gate to the interior of the campus. As she stood anxiously clutching her bag, a car pulled up beside her, and in it, a dark, handsome guy leaned over and opened the passenger side door.

"I know you're going my way, and it seems you're late, so..." He flashed a beautiful bright smile that later meant so much to her. Reluctantly, she got in, and he took off, driving in what she would come to know as his characteristic dare-devil style.

He was one of the most popular guys on campus. A final-year civil and environmental engineering student, he was tall, charming and intelligent. Although she had heard of him, she had never met or spoken to him and was a bit confused as to why he chose to give her a lift, out of all the people at the gate that day.

"I've seen you around, in case you're wondering." He said, almost like he was reading her thoughts.

"Okay."

His answer made her even more confused. Where and when did he see her? And more importantly, why did he notice her? She didn't go out and was not well known on campus. As he drove, he occasionally cast sideways glances at her with a devilish smile playing on his lips, which did nothing to quell her confusion or the strange feeling in her stomach. He was wearing a tight T-shirt, and she could see his chest and stomach muscles rippling under the fabric and the muscles on his arms flexing as he expertly manoeuvred the car through the morning campus traffic.

By the time they arrived at her department block, she was feeling quite light-headed. She couldn't remember when she agreed to be picked up after her afternoon classes. She was just eager to get away from his intoxicating presence, yet unable to resist seeing him again.

That became their daily routine for the rest of the week until Friday evening when he asked her out for a drink.

"Just a drink o, nothing else." He said, raising both hands in mock surrender, already knowing how reticent she would be and trying to forestall a refusal.

"After which you'll take me back home?"

"Straight back! No branching!" raising his right hand in a mock vow and with his disarming smile. Oh, that smile again, Hannatu thought as her breath caught in her throat. Thank God I'm dark-skinned, or he would see me blushing.

"Are you blushing?" he asked, his smile widening.

"Huh? Blushing? How?" she spluttered, and he burst out laughing.

Embarrassed, she turned and opened the car door to leave, but he stopped her with his hand on her upper arm.

"Don't go, please."

His touch felt both dangerous and comforting at the same time, and she didn't know when she had started nodding in agreement. She closed the door, and he drove out of campus to a restaurant not too far away so she felt comfortable and not too close to school so they would most likely not run into any of her classmates. He was sensitive like that. She wondered if it was an act or if it was the real Femi Adewale, as this side of him was quite different from his reputation on campus.

They settled into their seats and ordered drinks, and she ended up having such a good time with him that when he dropped her off, she was the one who shyly asked, "Will I see you on Monday?"

"Oh, wild horses could not keep me away from you." He replied and thus began the best year of her life.

They soon became inseparable. She cried when he graduated, but he always came to visit every chance he got. When he went for his national service in Abuja, the days felt like weeks, and the weeks felt like months.

They married in 2010 and settled into their new life, and Hannatu could not believe how complete her life had become. They made plans, they talked, laughed and loved each other. Even when, after three years, they had no children, he protected her from his overbearing mother. The more his mother pushed, the more he fought for her.

When she eventually got pregnant in 2014, she was overjoyed, and when her baby girl, Jamila was born beautiful, healthy and strong, her joy was complete. Femi doted on the child, taking time off work to spend as much time as he could helping Hannatu with the baby, to the point where his colleagues started teasing him. Femi didn't mind, proudly wearing the toga of whatever nickname they gave him.

That was their life until 2017 when Femi quit his job with the construction company he had worked in since he graduated and started his own business. Hannatu was sceptical about this move, especially the timing, but Femi was insistent. Things became strained between them for the first time in their relationship, so Hannatu let it go for peace.

Femi got several small contracts and made a decent living, with Hannatu working as an executive assistant to the chairman of a large chain of hotels in Victoria Island. As Femi's business grew, he started chasing bigger contracts through contacts he had made during his service year in Abuja.

Unfortunately, Abuja was a different kettle of fish, and things tended to move much slower. His existing business suffered as he chased that one big contract and their finances dwindled. They had to dig into their reserves, especially as Jamila had started school.

Their dwindling finances and the state of Femi's business also affected their relationship. Femi became withdrawn and started drinking and staying out late. Hannatu tried to be as supportive as possible by being patient and encouraging, but her efforts were rebuffed. By January

2020, she seemed excited only when he was about to go to Abuja. Hannatu put it down to the expectation of success in the contract discussions with the government officials he would see.

****

Femi had been in Abuja for two weeks, the first time their landlady had called her. It was unusual as she usually dealt more with Femi than her. Also, when she had spoken to him earlier that day, he didn't give her any message for the landlady. Their relationship was still strained, and she didn't know what to do about it.

The landlady kept calling back-to-back, and although Hannatu was trying to prepare dinner for herself and Jamila, on the fourth time, she answered and snapped, "Madam Landlady, what is it? Are we owing you? Why are you harassing me with all these calls?"

"Ah ah, Hannatu, are we fighting? I have important information I wanted to share with you all. Femi also didn't answer his phone. Is it a bad thing for me to call you?" The landlady replied over the phone testily.

"Hmm, okay, ma, don't be upset..." Hannatu tried to mollify her.

"No, no, it's okay! You young girls of these days think you can just talk to people anyhow you like. Anyway, my sources in Abuja told me the government would declare a nationwide lockdown! So you all need to stock up."

The landlady hung up abruptly before Hannatu could respond, so she quickly called Femi, who confirmed.

"Yes, check the news. They are talking about it on Channels Television now."

As she entered the sitting room to change the channel, Jamila played with a doll while watching cartoons. As Hannatu picked up the remote to change the channel, Jamila started crying.

"Ah, Jamila, please, na, I just need to check something", she admonished the child. However, Jamila kept sulking, so Hannatu pulled her to herself and gave her the phone to talk to her dad as she read the scrolling headlines on the screen.

Breaking news: President Muhammadu Buhari has announced a lockdown in Abuja, Lagos and Ogun to prevent the further spread of the coronavirus COVID-19. All movement in these areas will be prohibited for fourteen days from 11 pm Monday, March 30, 2020, and citizens have been ordered to stay at home. Authorities have instructed for all interstate travel to be postponed as well. Non-essential businesses and offices within these locations will be fully closed during this period.

Hannatu stared at the screen, feeling both shocked and worried. She took the phone back from Jamila.

"Femi, they are saying there is a lockdown with effect from this week." She was pacing by now.

"Yes, I saw it." He replied.

"So, what is going to happen now? Airlines will be grounded, so I suggest you come back tomorrow?"

"No, na, this is Nigeria. There will always be a way to travel. So, don't worry yourself. And in any case, I'm really close to meeting with the perm sec, so I can't come back immediately."

"Really, Femi!? So what will happen if the government effects a total nationwide lockdown? What would happen to us, I mean to us, me and Jamila? We don't know how long it would last..."

"Ah ah, what do you mean? Am I dead? I'm here na..."

"But that's the point. You're not here, you're there!"

There was an uncomfortable pause before Hannatu said. "I have to get back to cooking. Do you want to talk to Jamila again?"

"No, it's okay, go and do what you need to do. I'll talk to her tomorrow. Good night." With that, Femi hung up.

Hannatu stared at her phone in disbelief. She was so angry. When did they become like this?

****

It was a cold rainy night, and Hannatu was sitting at the table looking through her account on her banking app and comparing the statement with receipts and notes. She had just put Jamila to bed. She was getting more anxious about her finances every day. She realised she could not continue spending the way she was without encountering problems. She grabbed her phone and dialled a number.

"Hello, Femi. Good evening. I don't know what to do anymore." She blurted out, almost in tears. "I don't have any money, and you're not here. I'm out of petrol for the generator and running low on power credits. I have to prioritise Jamila's food..." By this point, she had started sobbing.

"Hannatu, it's okay, take it easy. The lockdown is affecting everybody. Let's just manage what we have..."

"Manage?! Manage what, exactly? You are not here. You've been gone for over a month. The lockdown keeps getting extended and extended. I can't go to work as my job is non-essential. What am I going to do? I need my husband. I told you before this started to come back, but you refused. You insisted on staying. You still didn't meet the perm sec and you can't come back. I'm tired, Femi. I just don't know what to do anymore," she resumed, sobbing.

"Hannatu, it's really late. I can't deal with this right now."

"Really, Femi!? You can't deal with this now? So, when is a good time to deal with your wife and child running out of food and maybe thrown out of our home? When, Femi!?"

"I said not now, Hannatu! I have to sleep now. I'll call you tomorrow." He hung up.

Hannatu sat there with her head bowed, crying. As much as she rationalised Femi's behaviour, putting it down to the pressures of the business, she couldn't help but realise that their relationship had deteriorated significantly. She almost couldn't believe how bad things had become between them. She got up slowly, dragged herself to the front door and checked that it was securely locked. Then she switched off the lights, checked on Jamila in her room and went into her room, their room—her and Femi's room.

Heaving a deep sigh of frustration, she flopped down on the bed and started crying quietly, one hand holding her phone and the other wrapped around her body. As she cried, she thought of the good times. The bed now felt so empty. The whole house seemed to echo with his absence. Longing for him made her cry even harder as she thought of his touch, his gaze, his kiss.

She fell asleep and dreamt of Femi with her on the bed and them making love long into the night.

****

Hannatu, clearly agitated, was talking on her cell phone in the kitchen. "But Mummy, it's been three months! Other people have found ways to return to their families. What on earth is stopping Femi from finding his way back to Lagos?"

She was almost shouting. Her hair was unkempt, she wore no makeup, and she had chewed her fingernails to the quick.

"Take it easy, Hannatu. Do you want to give yourself high blood pressure?" Her mother replied on the other end of the phone, trying unsuccessfully to defuse the situation.

"Mummy, I have tried to be rational, I have reasoned with him, I have talked, I have begged, I have nagged, and still nothing. There is no reasonable excuse. He just says it's the lockdown, yet other people have found ways to beat it. Mummy, this is Nigeria, for God's sake! How can a man like Femi not be able to find a way to come back to his family?" Raising her voice by the last statement.

"Hannatu, calm down!" her mother's voice had also gone up to match Hannatu's. "He is a man. Are you going to kill yourself? And what if he doesn't come back? Or he tries to do something illegal, and he is kidnapped on the road or dies in the process? What would you say then? The world won't stop because you want to sleep with your husband! Ah ah! Every day, Femi this, Femi that!" There was a pause while they both calmed down. "I've told you, he will come back when it is safe. Just take care of your daughter in the meantime and remain prayerful that none of us catch this disease. Too many people are dying."

"Okay, Mummy, I've heard you." As she capitulated, she made a mental note not to talk to her mother again about any intimate aspects of her relationship with her husband. There was a knock on the front door. "I have to go now. There's someone at the door. It must be my neighbour, Jane. They're having a small party for her son."

"Okay. Enjoy yourself small. Remember to wear a mask and sanitise you and Jamila's hands regularly, please. I don't want to hear any stories that touch."

"Yes, Mummy. Bye for now." Hannatu ended the call and rushed out of her room, almost running into Jamila.

"Mummy, Auntie Jane is at the door. The party is starting, and we will be late." As she spoke, she grabbed Hannatu's hand and pulled her towards the door.

"I know, baby, but Mummy needs to shower first and dress up." Hannatu tried to protest and slow the forward movement to the front door.

"But you don't need to dress up. The party is for kids, not grown-ups." Jamila countered.

Hannatu was stumped by Jamila's logic, and she stopped, and a smile broke out on her tired face. She looked down at the insistent child. "Okay, you got me. I'll take you to the party and then come back and get ready. But you have to promise never to take off your mask."

"I promise, Mummy. See, I'm already wearing my mask. Can we go now, please?" came the impatient response.

"Okay, okay, let's go."

Jamila bounded ahead as they went outside their flat, shrieking through her mask. By the time Hannatu locked the door, she was already running down the stairs.

"Jamila, wait for me!" She tried in vain to stop her, but Jamila was already on the first floor and wasn't about to stop. Hannatu had no choice but to wear her mask and hurry after her.

At the Adebolas' apartment, she knocked, but the music playing inside was so loud that she doubted that anyone could hear her over the music and the shouts, shrieks and screams of the children, one of which was clearly Jamila, so she turned the door handle and pushed the door in. As she did, the door flew open, and Jane Adebola rushed out in a state of panic.

"Ah, so sorry…" Hannatu apologised, stepping back outside to make way for Jane.

"Oh, no, I'm sorry, it's my fault. I'm so sorry, come in, come in. I thought you were already here because I saw Jamila playing with the other kids."

"No, it's okay, you came out. You seem to be in a hurry. I hope all is well with the party."

"Oh, it's not o, it's not, my sister."

"Ah, ah, what happened? What's wrong?" Hannatu asked as Jane joined her in the hallway, closing the door behind her. There was a stool outside the door, with a big bottle of hand sanitiser for people to use before entering the apartment.

"It's the photographer I hired. He was supposed to have been here two hours ago. I've been calling and texting him, but there is no answer or response. The guy just ghosted me, and now I don't know what to do. I knew something would go wrong, and now, Hassan will blame me. Oh God, what do I do?"

Jane Adebola was a petite and pretty woman who always seemed to wear a frown that had formed a little v on her forehead. When Hannatu first met her, she thought she was unfriendly. She later discovered that she was a worrier who found the dark cloud in every silver lining. That was on a good day. Today, she just stood there, a study in misery, pacing back and forth, wringing her hands with the v on her forehead appearing deeper.

"Calm down. Maybe he's on his way, and his phone is on silent. Or he is on a bike, and it's noisy." Hannatu tried to reassure her.

"Maybe… maybe…"

"What of Hassan? Can't he use his phone and take the pictures?"

"Ah! No o, that won't work o. I want professional pictures. It's my son's fifth birthday, and I want everything to be perfect." Jane responded. She looked like she was about to start crying.

"You know what, give me a few minutes. I'll be back."

With that, Hannatu ran up the stairs back to her apartment. She quickly showered, grabbed her phone, a small tripod, and a ring light, and rushed back down.

Jane was still in the hallway, pacing and looking more agitated.

"What are you going to do?" She asked when she saw Hannatu with the gadgets.

"It's pictures you want, it's pictures you'll get. If you don't like them, you can delete them and not use them."

She didn't allow Jane to protest that she wasn't a professional photographer. So she went in, set up her phone camera, adjusted the settings to a pro mode and started taking pictures. She took a few pictures and showed them to her and her husband, Hassan.

"Ah, Hannatu, these are great pictures. I didn't know you were a photographer." Hassan said in response to the pictures.

"I'm not o. I've just been playing around, taking pictures of my daughter. I watched some YouTube videos on camera settings, and I've been trying out the lessons. You like them?"

Jane looked at Hassan, and when he smiled happily, she heaved a huge sigh of relief and hugged Hannatu, whispering, "You're a lifesaver."

"Ah, you should open an IG page and start posting these pictures. They're very good." Hassan continued, obviously very impressed.

"Ah, they're not that good, na, haba. But thanks for the vote of confidence." She smiled, happy that she could help her neighbour with something she had been doing as a hobby to pass the time during lockdown.

With a boost of confidence, Hannatu spent the next few weeks focusing on the YouTube training videos, learning about camera angles, shutter speed, lighting, etc. and practising with Jamila. She borrowed money from her mother, sold her beat-up car and ordered professional equipment, including a Canon 5D Mark III camera, lens, electronic flash and a basic kit. She also learned how to edit pictures using Adobe Premier Pro and Photoshop. The more she took photographs and experimented, the better the quality of the finished work and the more confident she became. By this time, Jane had become her biggest supporter and cheerleader.

After experimenting, she felt confident enough to start taking pictures of the neighbours' children and posting them on her new Instagram page, Captured Moments. She converted a portion of her sitting room to a mini studio and began charging for her photographs, starting a small but niche business for child photography, especially newborn babies.

****

Hannatu and Jane were sitting in Hannatu's flat, looking through the comments on the Captured Moments business page on her phone. By this time, she had garnered over one thousand followers, and the comments were generally very positive and encouraging.

As they read and laughed, she got a text message of a credit alert into her bank account, and although her countenance remained unchanged, Jane noticed she became quieter and sad. Jane kept quiet and waited for Hannatu to say something. Even before the lockdown, she knew of Hannatu's challenges in Femi's absence. She could not understand why he had not returned to Lagos even after the partial lifting of travel restrictions. But she did not say anything because it was a sore subject for Hannatu, so she didn't want to ask how things were between them. They sat in awkward silence, the happiness of the room sucked out by that one text message.

"Femi sent some money. I guess things are beginning to look up. I'll have to go and get some groceries then. Should I get anything for you?" Hannatu said, standing up.

Jane understood that Hannatu needed to be left alone, so she quickly got up. "Oh, no, I'm fine, thanks. I'll come and see you tomorrow." Jane responded as she started walking towards the door. She stopped, turned and hugged Hannatu tight. "Everything will be alright. It will all work out, don't worry."

Hannatu nodded quietly, holding back tears. She forced a smile and hugged Jane back. "I'll see you later, and please give Hassan my regards." She walked Jane to the door. "Bye." As she closed and locked the door, her face crumpled, and the tears, hot tears of pain and frustration poured down her face.

****

Hannatu was in a rare good mood. She had finally landed a big client. This lady saw her page on Instagram and sent her a direct message. Her baby was one month old, and they wanted to take professional pictures. She was willing to pay her five hundred thousand naira to come to Parkview estate in Ikoyi and take the pictures at her house. The woman had transferred a fifty per cent deposit of half of the amount to her, which blew her away. This woman must be wealthy. She was already dreaming of all the new big clients she would get through this woman. She was determined to do the best job she had ever done.

She sang to herself as she prepared her equipment. She checked her batteries and memory cards, tripods, screens, etc. There was no room for error today. Satisfied that all was in order, she called a cab and set off. As the cab drove from Thomas Estate, Ajah, and across the Lekki Ikoyi Bridge into Parkview, Hannatu reminisced on how her life had changed over the past three months. She looked wistfully at the large, opulent buildings and luxury apartments, wondering at the lives of the people within them. *Well, I'll soon be meeting one of them*, she thought with a rueful smile.

At the Parkview gate, she gave the name and number the lady had given her and was granted access as the security men directed her where to go. The address was a block of luxury apartments with standby power generators, security and uniformed maids! She was met in front of the main entrance by a maid who helped her unload her equipment, led her into the flat and showed her where to set up in the outer sitting area. She looked around and was impressed by the simple elegance of the apartment and its furnishings. She wondered how beautiful the main sitting room and the rest of the apartment would be.

"Madam will join you in a minute." Her thoughts were interrupted by the maid.

"Oh, okay, that's fine." Hannatu checked her watch to ensure she arrived on time for the appointment. She had timed it so she wasn't late but also not too early so that she seemed professional and not desperate. So, fifteen minutes early, she was set up in ten minutes with five to spare. Now, to wait. She used the time to load her camera and do one more check of her equipment.

"Oh, hello, you must be Captured Moments." Hannatu turned round to see a lovely woman in her late twenties or early thirties walking towards her with her hand outstretched. She was very well dressed, her hair and makeup expertly done, and her perfume smelled rich.

"Good day, ma. My name is Hannatu, and I am from Captured Moments Photography. We take the best pictures of babies, and I'll ensure we capture this wonderful moment for you and your family."

The woman smiled sweetly. "Hannatu, that's a very nice name. Call me Moji. And you are so pretty. When I saw your page, I expected someone... well, not looking like you. You know what they say about those who hide behind the lens." They laughed together at the implication of her statement.

Hannatu thought they had got off to a great start, and her confidence was growing by the second. Then, a second maid walked in with the baby in her arms, and Moji took him from her.

"And here's our young prince sleeping peacefully."

"Oh, he's lovely, so handsome," she said, genuinely happy for Moji. And the baby was gorgeous. She was already planning poses and positions for the pictures when the maid asked if they were ready to start, as Oga needed to know if he should come down.

"I'm ready when you are," Hannatu said with a cheerful smile. "For the first position, you can sit here holding the baby and let me take some test shots." She pointed to the chair, and Moji sat down. She adjusted her dress, went back to the camera on the tripod and took a few shots. She made some adjustments to her settings and snapped a few more. She then took the camera off the tripod and walked over to show Moji the pictures on the camera LCD screen.

"Oh, these are nice, very nice. Junior looks so angelic sleeping." Moji replied happily.

"Yes, he does. I just want to take pictures of him all day long." Hannatu replied to an even broader smile from Moji.

"Oh, here comes my husband. I can't wait for him to see the beautiful pictures you just took."

Hannatu turned round smiling to see Moji's husband and stopped dead in her tracks. The room suddenly became cold and hot at the same time. Her vision dimmed as her head felt like a vice was squeezing it as she screamed. "Femi!" She tried to move, but the shock was so much that she stumbled. She quickly reached out, grabbed a chair and sat down, never taking her eyes off him. Femi stood rooted to the spot as a range of emotions flashed on his face: bewilderment, confusion, anger and a coldness she had never seen in his eyes. He looked from Hannatu to Moji and back, eyes darting like a caged animal.

Moji looked from one to the other, mouth open in confusion. Her confusion quickly gave way to comprehension as she realised what was happening.

Hannatu, overcoming her shock, lunged upward and forward at Femi, slapping him and clawing at his face. Her movement was so sudden that he had no time to react. He fell back under the ferocity of her attack, struggling to protect himself. Moji screamed, and between her and the maid, they succeeded in pulling Hannatu off him. He was already bleeding from a gash on his left cheek.

"Why? Why did you lie and leave your family?" Hannatu screamed at Femi as she struggled with Moji and the maid. Turning to Moji, "So you! It was you!" With that, she turned her fury to Moji. At this, Femi jumped forward, and the three of them were able to finally restrain Hannatu and force her down on a chair.

Heaving with exertion and anger, Hannatu looked from Femi to Moji, shaking her head, her head filled with so many conflicting thoughts.

"I'm sorry, I didn't know he had a wife at first." Moji started talking. "I didn't know he had another family. I only found out much later, but he assured me you wanted to leave him and were no longer sleeping together. His mother set us up, and we did traditional rites after I got pregnant. My family would never allow an abortion. I'm sorry, I'm just rambling..." She shook her head and stopped talking.

Hannatu kept looking at Femi while he sat with his head hanging.

"Do you have nothing to say to me? Are you just going to sit there? What do I tell your daughter?! That her father had been in Lagos all this time? Femi, what did I do to you? How could you do this to me? To your daughter? Femi, why?"

"I didn't plan this. I never planned to hurt you or Jamila," he finally stuttered. Hannatu scoffed at the mention of her daughter's name. "But what happened, happened. I've been thinking of how to tell you, finding the right time to tell you and break things off amicably..."

"Amicably? In which universe did you think this would end amicably? Eh, Femi?" She had gotten up, hands clenched into fists. "You know what, I can't deal with this."

She took a deep breath and turned to Moji, "Madam Moji, I came here to do a job. I want to get on with it if you don't mind."

"Er... I'm. I'm sorry, I'm not sure..." Moji stuttered. "Under the circumstances, I'm not sure that would be appropriate."

"Well, in that case, please send me your account details so I can return your money, less late cancellation charges."

With that, she turned and angrily started dismantling her equipment. Femi, Moji and the maid stood and watched awkwardly as she packed her stuff and started walking towards the door, with the maid helping her carry some.

"Hannatu, I'm sorry," Femi called out as she got to the door.

She turned with her hand on the door handle. Struggling to hide her pain and not break down in front of them, she forced a fake smile.

"Goodbye." She gave them one last look and walked out.

The maid helped her to the road, where she called a cab. She broke down and let the tears pour down her face only after the cab began her trip and she was on her way home.

Hannatu woke up screaming. The room was dark and hot. Her mother rushed into the room, switched on the light and rushed to her bedside. Hannatu burst into tears and started sobbing deep, heart-wrenching sobs.

"Hannatu, it's okay. Don't cry, my daughter. Everything will work out." Her mother tried to console her.

The door opened, and Jamila came in, rubbing her eyes. "Mummy, what's wrong? Why are you crying? Did anything happen to Daddy?" Hannatu wailed even louder at these innocent questions, and Jamila rushed onto the bed, hugged her mother and started crying. All three of them cried together, Jamila in fright and confusion, Hannatu with the pain of betrayal and her mother with the helplessness of her daughter's pain.

****

It had been two weeks since the incident in Ikoyi and the revelation of Femi's betrayal and double life. Hannatu had been going through the various stages of grief. She and her mother sat on the couch in the sitting room, talking.

"Three hundred thousand naira!" Hannatu exclaimed angrily. "Three hundred thousand after almost three months. That's all he ever sent. And all the while, he was living in Ikoyi with his other wife. Mummy, you need to have seen the house." She got up from the chair and started pacing back and forth, hands clenched into fists and seething with rage.

"You have described it to me. Femi did not do well." Her mother replied quietly.

Hannatu carried on as if she did not hear her mother. "Come home, no! Send money for upkeep, no! Call me, let me know how you're doing, no! Okay, I'm nobody to you, talk to your daughter, you're busy! Lockdown restrictions have eased. Come back to your family, story! Then you send me three hundred thousand naira that I should do what with? Ah, Femi..." she burst into tears. "And all the while, he was less than ten kilometres away, living and enjoying life in Ikoyi. Did I mention the house?"

"Yes, my daughter, you did."

"Beautiful house, Mummy. Beautiful wife and his son..." and the tears resumed.

"My daughter, come and sit down, please. Come, come."

Hannatu walked back to the couch and sat down beside her mother.

"What did I ever do to Femi to make him treat me like this? What did I do? Mummy, tell me, what did I do? Was this my fault?"

"No, no, my daughter, it was not your fault at all."

"Then why? Why, Mummy? I'm losing my mind. I just want to understand why. What did I do? Why did I not see it? When I think back, all the signs were there. How could I have been so blind?"

"It's not your fault."

"So, what could I have done to stop it?"

"There's nothing you could have done. A man would always do what a man chooses to do."

"But..."

"But nothing, Hannatu. Nothing. He did this! It's all on him. There's nothing you could have done."

"Nothing?"

"Nothing!"

They sat together in silence for a while.

"Meanwhile, his family knew. They knew about the other woman. They call her their wife. Moji is 'their wife,' and what does that make me?" She smiled, a smile of deep pain as silent tears continued to streak down her face. "They knew, they supported him, all because to them, I am not Yoruba, and I didn't have a son."

Her mother put her arm around her shoulder and just rubbed her upper arm.

"I wonder how long he had been lying to me. Was there even ever a contract in Abuja?"

"Hannatu, it's enough! You can't go on like this. You're driving yourself crazy, and your daughter is beginning to avoid you. You have to snap out of it." Her mother turned her around, held her by the shoulders at arm's length and shook her. "You need to see a therapist and my pastor. You have to take back your life. Femi is gone. You are now a single mother of a beautiful and intelligent young girl who depends on you for everything. You must fight back, recover your dignity and self-respect, and move forward. I don't want to see you weeping about that man anymore. Are we clear?"

"Yes, Mummy, I hear you."

"Okay, go and shower. I'll make something for you to eat, and we will talk about your next steps." Her mum got up and started walking to the kitchen.

"Okay, Mummy. Thank you for everything." She got up and walked out of the room.

****

Hannatu and her mother walked out of an office building on Akin Adesola Street in Victoria Island with Jamila in tow. They had a lawyer with them, and they talked in quiet tones.

"With this legal separation agreement, you and your daughter get a regular monthly upkeep, in addition to him paying for your accommodation. You can file for the final divorce once the legal separation period is complete." The lawyer, Barrister Ogundipe, seemed quite happy that the discussions had progressed without undue contention and wrapped up quickly. He was also happy that he had included Hannatu's legal costs as part of the settlement.

"I understand. Thank you very much, Barrister." Hannatu replied, relieved that this part of the process was concluded. It was still surreal to her. She could not believe that the man across the table from her was the same man she had fallen in love with, married and planned to spend the rest of her life with. How did it all fall apart? How did he go from the love of her life to this cold stranger who couldn't look at her anymore?

"Daddy!"

Hannatu turned towards the direction Jamila was looking at. At the same time, Femi, hearing Jamila's voice, turned and saw them. For a moment, they all stood still, looking at each other. Femi started walking towards them and tried to beckon Jamila, but Hannatu held her back. Jamila looked at her mother with a questioning look, but Hannatu looked down at her and shook her head.

Looking up at Femi standing with his arms extended towards Jamila, Hannatu shook her head and put her arm firmly around Jamila's shoulder.

"No, Femi, no. You don't get to talk to her. Goodbye."

Femi turned away, joined Moji in their Mercedes Benz and drove off. Hannatu and her mother looked at each other, smiled at Jamila, turned and walked into a new life filled with possibilities.

The End.

Michael W. Ndiomu *is a storyteller of authentic African stories for a global audience using writing and filmmaking as media. He graduated with a degree in mathematics and worked as an investment banker for two decades before starting his journey in the creative space. Michael attended the prestigious New York Film Academy and later set up and ran a cinema and* *film production company in Lagos. He co-produced the runaway hit* The Origin: Madam Koi Koi, *currently streaming on Netflix.*

Edited by Ibiso Graham-Douglas

We Shall Rise

Obari Gomba

AS WE LOOK AT THE OPEN JAWS OF THIS FEARSOME
pestilence, we see that the earth has always
known pain and bliss, unevenly spaced out.

The fingers of time grow and wither,
bloom and wilt. The wild eyes of nature
can be as unkind as the range of its hands.

Yes, nature's beauty has its ugly ways. Yes,
nature wars always with human nurture
and the fierce forces of their temper sow
distemper.

So, brethren, the earth has never
failed to swallow us, but it has
never swallowed
all of us. Not at once. Between nature's wrath
and the treachery of human power, haughty
knowledge causes us to fall too often.
We always fall and we always rise.

The limit of nature's might over us
is like the limit
of our folly over our resilience. On this earth,
we shall overcome the terrors

that come upon us.

This pestilence will not be the end of us.
We shall rise if we fall to rise, fall to rise again.

Obari Gomba (PhD), *winner of both the Nigeria Prize for Literature and the PAWA Prize for African Poetry, is an Honorary Fellow in Writing of the University of Iowa (USA) and the Associate Dean of Humanities at the University of Port Harcourt (Nigeria). He has been the TORCH Global South Visiting Professor and Visiting Fellow at All Souls College, University of Oxford (UK). He is a two-time winner of the Best Literary Artiste Award and the First Prize for Drama of the English Association of the University of Nigeria, Nsukka. His works include* Guerrilla Post *(Winner of ANA Drama Prize),* For Every Homeland *(Winner of ANA Poetry Prize),* Thunder Protocol *(Winner of ANA Poetry Prize), among others.*

Edited by Ibiso Graham-Douglas

Editor's Note

I lost my mother and two uncles to Covid in 2020 and 2021. This book emerges from a deeply personal sense of necessity to document that time in history, especially living in a country where disbelief and conspiracy theories about the virus and pandemic were rife and where today, the notion of COVID is largely dismissed.

While official records detail cases, deaths, recoveries and vaccination efforts, I wanted to capture our collective perceptions and experiences of the COVID era, defining it for our people and a generation.

I sought to document the diverse ways people encountered the virus, how it disrupted lives, and yet how resilience prevailed. I realised that my suffering was not only associated with death but in other ways that lives were interrupted.

This compilation features new and seasoned voices, offering a glimpse into the kaleidoscope of Nigerian COVID experiences. My immense gratitude goes to the authors who embraced this vision and graciously contributed. I have also written a story on cosmetic surgery, a subject I think we consider too lightly amidst our derelict health sector. These stories and poems do not encompass the entirety of these experiences—such a task would be impossible—but rather, they affirm that COVID indeed happened—in Nigeria, altering lives in complex myriad ways.

In the words of Obari Gomba, "*This pestilence will not be the end of us. We shall rise if we fall to rise, fall to rise again.*"

Acknowledgements

My heartfelt gratitude extends to the remarkable authors—Obari Gomba, Dolapo Marinho, Olukorede S. Yishau, Michael Afenfia, Shehu Zock-Sock, Chimeka Garricks and Michael W. Ndiomu. Your invaluable contributions and incredible patience during our collaborative process have been a true gift. I am thankful for each of you and feel immensely blessed to have had the opportunity to work alongside such talented individuals.

Thank you to Bukola Akinyemi, book club host and reviewer now turned friend. Dr Mamsallah Faal-Omisore, thank you for your guidance with the medical terminology and support in so many other areas.

My Paperworth Books team—Esther, Christianah, Onyinyechi, Kathy and Lesia. Thank you for all your hard work.

Thank you to my sister-friends, Ituen, Awongo, Konyinsola, Bolanle and my bff, Ogochukwu. I appreciate all your help and support in making this book a reality.

Thank you to my family—Daba, Semabo, Owanari, Telema, Bikiya, Crystal and Natasha. Knowing I can always count on you all is a blessing.

Lastly, to the giver of all good gifts and my constant Helper, God Almighty, Thank you, Lord.

About the Editor

Ibiso Graham-Douglas is a seasoned publisher and book industry professional with over two decades of expertise. Her impact is evident across the literary landscape, with a portfolio of titles across various genres. As the founder of Paperworth Books, Ibiso firmly believes in the inherent richness of African narratives, considering them fundamentally universal and complete in their own right. She has a BA in Financial Services and Politics, an MA in Publishing, and an MBA in International Business Management.

Other Titles by Contributors

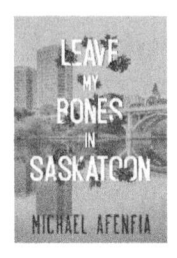

Leave My Bones in Saskatoon by Michael Afenfia

Through the eyes of Owoicho, a television presenter seeking a better life for himself and his family, Leave my Bones in Saskatoon spans two cultures and continents. It is honest, heartfelt and enlightening. The story begins with Owoicho's good news. He can't wait to tell his family that their permanent residency application to Canada was successful. But while he was in Abuja, happy about this breakthrough, somewhere on the outskirts of Makurdi, a dark and troubling event threatens to torpedo all the plans he and his wife, Ene, made to move the family to Saskatoon.

Rain Can Never Know by Michael Afenfia

Rain Tamuno is a brilliant young employee in Edozie Express, the largest construction company in the Niger Delta. Befriended by Chief Rowland Edozie, owner of the company, she experiences a meteoric rise in her career.

As her professional life flourishes, her personal life descends into turmoil. Forced to confront a traumatic episode from her past, Rain cannot come to terms with the fact that her mother chose her assailant over her. As she struggles to mend their fractured relationship, her relationship with David, her boyfriend, is threatened by her best friend, Annabel.

When sudden death occurs amid Chief Rowland Edozie's quest for a diabolical solution to a life-threatening problem, Rain's life is put at risk. As her world begins to crumble, she grapples with coming to terms with who her friends and foes are.
Rain Can Never Know is an intriguing story of love, lust, secrets and betrayal. It is about family, friends and faith.

Mechanics of Yenagoa by Michael Afenfia

Ebinimi, star mechanic of Kalakala Street, is a man with a hapless knack for getting in and out of trouble. Some of his troubles are self-inflicted: like his recurring entanglements in love triangles; and his unauthorised joyriding of a customer's car which sets off a chain of dire events involving drugs, crooked politicians, and assassins. Other troubles are caused by the panorama of characters in his life, like: his sister and her dysfunctional domestic situation; the three other mechanics he employs; and the money-loving preacher who has all but taken over his home. The story is fast-paced with surprising twists and a captivating plot – a Dickenesque page-turner. This is Ebinimi's story but it is about a lot more than him. It is an exploration of the dynamics between working-class people as they undertake a colourful tour of Yenagoa, one of Nigeria's lesser-known cities, while using humour, sex, and music, as coping mechanisms for the everyday struggle. It is a modern-classic tale of small lives navigating a big city.

Tomorrow Died Yesterday by Chimeka Garricks

In Port Harcourt at the height of the kidnap of oil workers in the Niger Delta, a kidnapping goes awry, and four lives are reconnected. Douye aka Doughboy the career militant responsible for the crime, Amaibi the gentle university professor/eco-warrior accused. Kaniye the lawyer turned restaurateur who tries to get him off and Tubo an amoral oil company executive. Against a backdrop of corrupt practises, failed systems and injustice, these four friends tell the story of oil in a region and its effects on local communities and the Nigerian larger society.

A Broken People's Playlist by Chimeka Garricks

A Broken People's Playlist is set to the soundtrack of life, comprised of twelve music-inspired tales about love, the human condition, micro-moments, and the search for meaning and sometimes, redemption. It is also Chimeka Garricks's love letter to his native city, Port Harcourt, introducing us to a cast of indelible characters in these loosely interlocked tales.

There is the teenage wannabe-DJ eager to play his first gig even as his family disastrously falls apart—who reappears many years later as an unhappy middle-aged man drunk-calling his ex-wife; a man who throws a living funeral for his dying brother; three friends who ponder penis captivus and one's peculiar erectile dysfunction; a troubled woman who tries to find her peace-place in the world, helped by a headful of songs and a pot of ginger tea.

Edited by Ibiso Graham-Douglas

GRIT by Obari Gomba

Obari Gomba, a multiple award-winning writer, is an Honorary Fellow in Writing of the University of Iowa (USA). He has been TORCH Global South Visiting Professor and Visiting Fellow at All Souls College, University of Oxford (UK). He is presently the Associate Dean of Humanities at the University of Port Harcourt in Nigeria. In 2018, his *Guerilla Post* won the Association of Nigerian Authors Drama Prize. His poetry collection, *The Lilt of the Rebel*, won the PAWA Prize for African Poetry in 2022.

Free Troubles by Obari Gomba

Free Troubles: A Writer's Eyes on the World is a collection of beautifully written essays that x-rays, critiques and parodies the ills of modern day society.

Obari Gomba employs tropes of satire and social commentary, pyrotechnics of wit, beauty of language, diversity of style, force of imagination and experimentation, and first-person point of view to give immediacy to his context and content. The essays risk everything, through a blend of aesthetics and insightfulness, to compel us to pay attention to the intractable problems of existence. It is an intense examination of our culture, a critique of our social structures, a show of irreverence towards abusive authority, and a resistance against the normalisation of evil.

After the End by Olukorede S. Yishau

Idera's world crumbles when her husband, Demola, dies. As she battles with this reality, she is met with a shocking discovery. A woman appears at her door with a child in hand—Demola's son.

The love of her life, the man whom she felt could do no wrong by her and her children, had betrayed her.

Idera is whisked into a place of uncertainty, scrutinising everything she's ever known to be true, unbeknownst to her that even more tragedy and surprises await. She must fight to save herself and her children.

Vaults of Secrets by Olukorede S. Yishau

The stories in Vaults of Secrets flirt with the limits of freedom and bondage. They are means through which award-winning journalist Olukorede S. Yishau examines the nature of man and his ability to make choices and live with the repercussions. The complex, beautifully drawn characters unveil the many grotesques of human life and shed light on their dark recesses exposing their weaknesses. Heartrending, luminous, and indelible, this is an astoundingly audacious collection of short stories.

Printed in Great Britain
by Amazon